FROST AND FOUND

AVA HILL

Cover art and design by Melissa Arancibia @Artzxmel

PLAYLIST

Who Knew - P!nk

Disconnected - P!nk

A Nonsense Christmas - Sabrina Carpenter

This Love (Taylor's Version) - Taylor Swift

'tis the damn season - Taylor Swift

When We Were Young - Adele

The Other Side - Ruelle

This holiday season, we all deserve a hot, older cowboy to be obsessed with us.

Especially if he has a little bit of a breeding kink.

ONE
SCARLETT

Men are as irrelevant to a woman's existence as a laugh track is in a sitcom, yet my sister still insists on marrying one. Luckily, Luke happens to be the perfect person for her, so that makes him acceptable in my books. It also helps that they've been together since they were teenagers and I've known him half my life.

I shiver in my coat as I watch my sister pacing back and forth twenty feet away from me, talking animatedly with her fiancé while I fill the car with gas.

"You'd think they haven't talked to each other in weeks rather than the mere five hours it took for us to fly from New York to Calgary," our youngest sister, Sadie, says from the back seat of the car. Her window is rolled down and she's watching Sienna with the curiosity of a cat.

"She's going to forget us as soon as she's married," I say.

"She was just using us to make herself look good," Sadie agrees.

I nod. "We're the ugly stepsisters and she's Cinderella."

"Are you two talking trash about me?" Sienna asks, walking back to us.

"No," Sadie and I say at the same time. We smirk at each other as Sienna rolls her eyes knowingly and sticks her tongue out at us.

"Let's see how you act when you're marrying the love of your life," she says.

That's never going to happen.

I brush off the bitter thought as the pump clicks under my hand and I remove it.

"Does anyone want snacks?" I ask, grabbing my purse from the car. It's a good thing we rented an SUV at the airport because we packed like it's the apocalypse and not a two-week destination wedding. We gave our rental to our parents', so they didn't have to stop for gas and took theirs, instead. Hence the pitstop.

"I'll come. I have to pee, anyway," Sadie says.

She grabs her hat, pulling it low over her brown hair. We all got our mother's brown hair and her features, a fact my mother loves. The day I showed up with lavender hair was the day my mother decided I didn't love her. It's taken her five years to come around and realize the lavender is not going anywhere anytime soon.

"Why is it so cold?" Sienna says, tucking her hands into her jacket pocket.

Sadie gives her a look. "You're the one who wanted to get married in the middle of nowhere Alberta, in December."

We enter the store, and I make a beeline to the snack's aisle, grabbing a bag of our favorite chips.

"Cedar Creek Ranch isn't in the middle of nowhere," Sienna protests. "Silverpine is only two hours from Calgary."

"In the Rockies," Sadie says.

Sienna and Sadie get in line for the washroom still arguing about this destination wedding while I pay for the gas and our snacks. We love Sienna and her choice to get married anywhere she wants, but we'd be terrible younger sisters if we didn't tease her about it.

The photos Sienna showed us of Cedar Creek Ranch were so gorgeous they didn't even look real. A huge ranch nestled under the Rockies, the snow-covered mountains looking almost AI generated.

I couldn't have picked a better place for my sister to marry the love of her life.

I hand over the snacks to my sisters while I quickly use the washroom. Sadie takes over for the rest of the drive.

"I wonder if mom and dad are already there," Sienna says from the front seat.

"If they were, we'd be getting calls every ten minutes asking us where we are," I say.

"Ten minutes is being generous," Sadie adds with a laugh.

I wouldn't say our mother is a helicopter mom, but she's not *not* one. She's raised three, fearless daughters and supported us fully no matter what we wanted to do. She's also overprotective to the point where she tracks our location and if we're not where we are meant to be, she'll call us right away.

"I'm going to take a nap. Wake me up when we get there," I say.

I haven't had a proper night's sleep in almost three days because I've been busy with maid of honor duties. My eyes are already closing when I hear one of my sisters say that I'm going to miss the beautiful scenery.

I WAKE up with the slam of a car door and open my eyes to see the charming Inn we're parked in front of. It looks like an elaborate gingerbread house and immediately makes me think of a Christmas horror movie and this is Santa's village for the damned. I suddenly fear that if I go in, I'm not coming back out.

"Are you coming, sleepyhead?" Sadie asks, turning back to look at me.

I nod, covering my mouth to hide a yawn. We get out of the car and leave the luggage for later. Sienna is already walking ahead, climbing the porch steps. Sadie and I stand by the car, looking up at the massive mansion in front of us.

There's a huge Christmas tree on the porch and so many Christmas lights that even if they turn off the interior lights, the whole place will still be bright.

"This is like a Christmas horror movie," Sadie says, hooking her arm through mine.

"I thought the same thing!"

We shiver as we walk towards the porch. With the sun going down, it's somehow gotten colder. Sienna enters the Inn before us. A wooden plaque is hanging on the inside of the door with the Inn's name on it: The Honeysuckle.

Mom and Dad are in the lobby, talking to the old woman behind the counter. Mom is animatedly telling her all about Sienna's wedding. She looks up excitedly when the three of us walk in.

"There they are!"

Rushing over, Mom envelopes the three of us into a hug, as if she hasn't seen us in months rather than the couple of hours to took to get here. To be fair, we were all in a rush to get out of the airport and my parents have been in Calgary for over a week. This the first time we're having a proper conversation today. She squeezes us until we're breathless and crying for mercy. Dad is standing right behind her, waiting his turn.

I squeeze out of Mom's arms and give him a quick side hug. He and I are the same, we keep our emotions inside and our physical touch limited; we don't like people in our personal space.

"How was the flight?" Dad asks, his blue eyes crinkling at the corners as he pulls Mom away from my sisters.

"It was fine," I say. "Sadie got into a fight with another passenger."

My baby sister turns at the sound of her name, hazel eyes narrowed. Sienna and Sadie both got Mom's hazel eyes, and I got Dad's baby blues. There's a running joke in my family that with my eyes and lavender hair, I look like a witch.

"That man was rude! I apologized for bumping into him and he glared at him. What kind of person doesn't accept an apology?"

"A rude one," Mom agrees.

I'm not saying the man wasn't rude. I just wouldn't have picked a fight with him, which is a lot coming from me because apparently I fight with people for no good reason.

"Did you get the chance to talk to Luke?" Mom asks.

Sadie and I automatically make kissing noises because we wouldn't be good sisters if we didn't tease Sienna. Our older sister blushes, but the glow on her is undeniable. She's so happy it's bursting out of her like sunshine. I want to wrap her up and protect her.

"Girls, be nice to your sister," Mom chides, though there's no anger behind her words.

"I did talk to Luke. He'll be here next week in time for the wedding festivities to begin," Sienna says.

The benefit of us working for ourselves means we were able

to come here two weeks in advance of the wedding, and Sienna and Luke will still have two weeks for their honeymoon.

Sienna works as a freelance graphic designer, Sadie is finishing her marketing degree while helping Mom and Dad at the family chocolate shop, and I'm a voice actor. Except the acting I do is for audio erotica and romance novels. I still haven't figured out how to tell people that part when they ask if they've heard me in anything. They hear voice acting and think animated movies.

Mom claps once. "Okay, let's get settled. Daddy and I found a nice restaurant for dinner. Why don't you girls freshen up and change and we'll meet back here in an hour?"

"Oh, can we go see Cedar Creek Ranch?" Sadie asks, eyes bright.

"I think that's a great idea," Mom says. "We can see the wedding venue."

"At this hour, they will probably be closed for an event," the old lady behind the counter adds. Her name tag reads Marion. She must be about my grandmother's age.

"Okay, that answers that question," Sienna says. "We have an appointment to go there tomorrow, anyway."

"It's much better in the light," Marion agrees.

With the decision made that we'll visit Cedar Creek Ranch tomorrow morning, my sisters and I get our luggage from the car and carry it up to our rooms. Sadie and I are sharing a room with a connecting door with Sienna's room. Our parents are across the hall.

While Sadie freshens up, I open the curtains and look out at the street below. I hadn't noticed at first, but every storefront on the street is decorated to the nines. It's like they're preparing to shoot a Hallmark movie here. It's so charming and quaint and it suits Sienna's personality perfectly.

I can imagine my sister living in this town and being happy

with the monotony. There's no way I'd ever fit in with these people. They are all probably so nice and kind, going out of their way to help people. I'm suspicious by nature so being nice and kind is like my third response when meeting someone.

It's a good thing I'd never consider moving to a small town. I leave the curtains open as Sadie walks out of the washroom and it's my turn to get ready for dinner.

TWO
SCARLETT

Ever since I was sixteen and started running track for my high school team, I've been waking up at six in the morning to go for a run. No matter where I am or what the weather is, my alarm goes off at six in the morning every day and I go for a run.

I'm moving around the room slowly, trying not to wake Sadie as I put on my shoes. She's pulled the blanket over her head so the only thing visible of her is her dark hair. I've got on my winter running gear and I make sure to grab my headphones and the room key before stepping out into the hallway.

As soon as I do, the door across the hall opens and my dad steps out. He's got his jacket and cap on, rubbing his hands together as he warms up.

"Daddy, you don't have to do this," I say. "I'm pretty sure Silverpine doesn't even have a criminal history."

You know how they say some men are just born to be girl dads? Well, my father is one of those men. He's probably participated in everything his daughters have wanted to do, whether that's running a marathon or hosting a princess tea party eight years in a row.

He wore the tiaras and the nail polish, picked out our prettiest dresses, and showed up for us in every way possible. Exhibit A, he's been waking up with me at 5 AM since I started running. He's not going to let his daughter run around the city unprotected.

"The day you get married, I'll pass the baton to your husband," he says.

"You're going to be stuck doing this for a long time because I don't trust any man enough to marry him."

Been there, done that, never plan on doing it again.

I shake off the bitter thought as we walk down the hallway.

"I'll be waking up with you as long as I live," Dad says.

"I'll take you up on that offer," I say.

We climb the stairs down to the ground floor and find it empty, except for Marion standing behind the counter. It smells sugary and cinnamony, and I immediately find the source to be the cinnamon buns that Marion has set out on the table along the front windows. Three different thermoses are set up as well for coffee, tea, and hot chocolate. The Christmas tree is lit up as it was last night and so are all the Christmas lights.

It's so warm and cozy, I almost falter on my way out the door.

Marion looks up as Dad and I walk into the lobby. She must be in her seventies, with hair that had gone white and kind brown eyes. Mom told me she was the owner of the Inn and that it had been in her family for generations. Her husband passed away two years ago and her step-grandsons helped her run the Inn, though she did the day-to-day work.

Mom would have gotten Marion's whole life story if we hadn't shown up and distracted her last night. She left her job ten years ago, but her investigative journalist skills were still strong.

"Good morning. Isn't it a little early to be up?" Marion smiled brightly.

"It's this one." Dad tilts his head toward me. "She goes on a run every morning, unless the weather is so temperamental it's safer to be inside. I can't have my daughter running around early in the morning."

Marion looks at me, brown eyes widening in surprise. "You're going running in this freezing weather? You know we have a small gym on site, maybe you should use it?"

It was zero degrees outside, so I wouldn't say it's freezing. The idea of a gym is tempting, especially since it will be warm, but I always grow restless on a treadmill. I need the open space, to breath fresh air, to feel like I'm running towards something rather than in place.

"Maybe I'll take you up on your offer tomorrow," I say. "I'm already dressed to go running outside."

"Let me make you a thermos of coffee to take with you," Marion says.

Getting out from behind the counter, she ambles to the kitchen and comes out a minute later with a big thermos of coffee and a bakery box of cinnamon rolls. Dad's eyes brighten with delight as he takes the loot of Marion's hands and thanks her profusely.

"You know you're not supposed to eat that," I say. His blood sugar was a little high during his last check-up and mom had put him on a strict diet. He'd lost like fifteen pounds since then.

"One isn't going to kill me," he says. He warms up the car and removes the snow which fell overnight while I warm-up.

It's freezing outside and still dark. Most shops are still closed, the streetlights are still on. The only shops open are the coffee shop/cafe down the road and the hardware store, both of which already have customers.

Dad and I map out a route that takes us through Cedar Creek Ranch and then I put on my headphones while he starts the car. Moving my body after sitting cramped in the plane and then the car yesterday feels amazing.

I start with a slow jog, Britney Spears pumping in my ears. As a kid I hated all activities which required me to be outside and around people. I was happier playing with my sisters or by myself, coloring the walls of our apartment or reading under a blanket. My sisters take after our mother and they're social butterflies, Dad and I are more reticent. Which is why this arrangement works for us. We both need time to ourselves to prepare for the day ahead, to clear our heads.

After my first mile, I can't even feel the cold anymore. I'm careful to avoid any snowy/slushy areas and it quickly becomes obvious that running in Silverpine in the winter is taking your life in your hands. It's a quiet town, a sharp contrast to my morning runs back in Brooklyn and Manhattan.

I lose myself in the rhythm of the music and the feel of my feet hitting the pavement. It doesn't take long before I've left the town behind me and I'm running down an unpaved road with snow piled along the sides and an open field around us, now covered in snow.

As the sun starts to rise, I become aware of something in my peripheral vision. I turn my head and see in the distance, there's someone riding a horse. They're too far away for me to make out any details, except for the fact that the rider is wearing a black cowboy hat riding a gorgeous black horse. The image of the rider against the stark white snow is striking.

I see the rider turn to look at me as the horse speeds up. Maybe it's my competitive side, but I can't stop as my feet push harder against the ground. I realize competing against a horse is insane, but I don't want to let that person win. I'm pushing faster and harder, running right alongside the horse and its rider.

My music is loud, but I still hear the honk of the car behind me. Dad is warning me not to do this because he knows that I can't let this competition go.

I stop abruptly when I hit a bend in the road and a gate blocks my way. I reach up to pull off my headphones. My heart drums wildly in my ears.

The rider pulls on the reins and the horse stops with a whiny. The rider and I just stare at each other across the distance. He's so far away that I can't make out his features, but I know he's looking at me. I can feel his eyes on me, which is so stupid because for all I know, he thinks I'm an idiot for competing against a horse.

Something keeps me rooted to the spot. Some inexplicable pull inside my chest which tells me to stay a minute, to breathe in the cold air, feel the sweat cool on my body.

I take a step forward.

Snow crunching under footsteps startles me and I turn around to see my dad walking towards me. The car is idling a few feet away.

"Angel, we should get back to your mom and sisters. You know they'll have a whole list of things planned."

I nod. "Okay, let's go."

Dad throws a look behind me at the horse and its rider before walking back to the car. I glance over my shoulder, and the rider lifts his black cowboy hat and tilts his head towards me.

I almost smile, almost. Until I remind myself that I'm only here for two weeks, and I'm also done with men.

Shaking my head, I turn and climb into the car.

"He's cute," Dad says.

I laugh, picking up a cinnamon roll. "You can't even see him."

Dad makes a three-point turn and starts driving back the way we just came.

"I can pick up on vibes. The next thing I know you'll be falling in love and moving to Silverpine."

I choke on my cinnamon roll. "There is no way I'm falling in love or moving to Silverpine. I'm probably going to be living at home when I'm sixty with you and Mom."

Dad hums quietly. "You say that now but the next thing you're going to say is that you're getting married."

It's a good thing he's teasing me because I don't have to tell him that's probably never going to happen. I've already fallen in love and had my heart broken once. It's not an experience I wish to repeat. No one tells you how hard it is to recover from a heartbreak when you thought that you met your soulmate.

I look in the side mirror and the horse and its rider are still there.

THREE
SCARLETT

My sisters and mother are already up and ready by the time Dad and I get back to the Inn. It hasn't been that long since I went running, but they're excited to go see Cedar Creek Ranch, and the place where my sister is going to get married.

I've done my research on Cedar Creek Ranch, and on the website, it's absolutely gorgeous. They took the photos against a backdrop of the Rocky Mountains, snow covered in the winter and with the sun dipping behind them in the summer, casting the sky into a beautiful rainbow of colors. Cedar Creek Ranch is a working ranch, but five years ago, they opened an event space which is on the huge property, but far away from any ranch work and the main house.

"Are we having breakfast? I'm starving," I say, after I've showered and changed into leggings and a sweater. I dry my hair and put it into rollers while I do my make-up.

"We're going to stop by the cafe on our way to the ranch," Sienna calls from her room. The door between our rooms is open. "They have another event tonight so we're catching them at a busy time but the coordinator said we can do a tour."

My stomach rumbles at the thought of breakfast. I'm more excited about breakfast than I am about seeing my sister's wedding venue. The idea of her getting married is melancholic because suddenly it's not going to be the three of us anymore. It's going to be me and Sadie, and Sienna and Luke. They're going to have a separate life that they make together and even though we will always be a part of it, there's going to be a divide we won't be able to bridge.

I can't let go of the thought that I am losing my sister. My therapist would tell me I'm catastrophizing, like I always do. I need to focus on the good, like my sister marrying the love of her life, a man we've known most of our lives.

"I'm starving," Sadie says, pushing in behind me. There isn't enough room in the washroom for the both of us. "Has your butt gotten bigger?" She struggles to move in front of me.

"It's definitely bigger than your pancake butt."

Sadie moves again as I'm in the middle of applying blush. My arm jostles and the wand moves over my cheek, spreading blush everywhere. Sadie and I freeze, staring at the streak of red on my face. I meet her hazel eyes in the mirror and Sadie shrieks.

"Mom!"

She rushes out of the washroom as I follow her. "Look what she's done!" I point to my cheek.

My parents, who are sitting in the chairs in our room, look up from their conversation and at my face.

"She was hogging the washroom!" Sadie complains.

"I'm trying to get ready!"

Sadie sits down on the armrest of Mom's chair and tries to hide behind our mother. At twenty-one, she's the youngest of us sisters, which means she gets away with a lot. Sienna is the oldest at thirty and like every eldest child, she's the responsible one. Then there's me, twenty-seven and the quintessential middle child, who always has to adjust.

"Girls, don't fight," Dad says, ever the peacekeeper. "Angel, why don't you finish getting ready?"

I give Sadie the stink eye as I walk back into the washroom. Wiping away the streak of blush, I reapply my base. Once I'm done, I pull on my knee-high boots and take my hair out of the rollers and I'm all set.

We grab breakfast to go and pile into one car as Sienna drives us to Cedar Creek Ranch.

As we get closer, the road starts to look familiar.

"This is where Scarlett saw her cowboy," Dad says, as Sienna turns the car down the same unpaved road I was running on earlier.

"Dad!" I exclaim, as my cheeks heat.

"Her wh-at?" Sadie and Sienna simultaneously, drawing out the word.

Knowing my sisters, they're never going to let it go.

"There was a man horse riding in the field when I was out running," I explain. "He's not my cowboy."

"There was very intense eye contact," Dad chimes in from the back.

Oh my god! I look out the window to hide my face. The thought of that man still made me squirmy so I'd rather not think about him.

"He was very far away," I say. "There wasn't any eye contact."

"Can you imagine if Scarlett finds the love of her life in the process of getting Sienna married?" Mom says.

I don't know how I was born into a family of romantics. Don't get me wrong. I like romance, I like the idea of falling in love. I wouldn't be able to do my job if I didn't. But I've been in love and just because someone says they love you doesn't mean they won't break your heart.

"I can guarantee you, I'm not going to meet the love of my life," I tell them.

Mostly because I've already met him, I don't add. I never really got around to introducing him to my family.

"Never say never," Sienna sings.

"Easy for you to say. You're marrying the boy you've been dating since high school," I say.

"Yeah, you don't get to opine about dating in this day and age when you've only dated one person," Sadie adds.

"Mom and Dad only dated each other," Sienna says.

"It was different in the ancient times," Sadie quips.

Sienna turns the car with the bend in the road and I notice the gate there has been opened.

"Did you hear that, Kate? Our daughters think we're old and decrepit," Dad says.

"Practically ready to be mummified," Mom jokes.

We drive for another mile before we finally see a paved driveway, parking lot, and a large building that resembles a ski lodge. Behind it, the Rockies rise in the clear blue sky. Sienna and Sadie let out an excited squeal.

Sienna parks the car, and we get out, breathing in the cold, clean sharpness of the icy mountain air. Sadie hooks her arm through mine as we walk up to the building.

Inside, it's warm and smells like Christmas. There's a big tree by the reception desk, mistletoe hanging over the door, Christmas music plays softly from a speaker. There's a woman behind the counter wearing a thick white sweater and black slacks, her hair twisted up into a bun.

She looks up when we walk in and smiles. "You must be the Monroes."

"That's us," Sienna says.

"Great! I'm Hannah and I'll be your guide," she walks around her desk. "Who's the bride?"

We all point at Sienna.

"We're trying to get rid of her," I say.

"She's so annoying," Sadie agrees.

Sienna rolls her eyes and sticks her tongue out at us. Hannah laughs and leads us further into the building.

"Welcome to Cedar Creek Lodge," Hannah says. "It was built in 1937 as a lodge for the rich and famous to get away from the real world and was shut down in 2005. We re-opened five years ago as an event space."

Hannah leads us through the lobby, which overlooks a terrace with a large hot tub.

"Are there any plans to open the lodge again?" Dad asks.

"Absolutely!" Hannah says, grinning. "Cedar Creek is a big property, and our new owner has a lot of plans for it. He hopes to have the lodge operational in the next two years, but there are a lot of technicalities he's working through."

She's practically got stars in her eyes when she speaks of this owner.

"You'll have access to the whole lodge during your big day. Your guests can hang out here or in the venue. We do have another two events scheduled for the same day, but they will be in the smaller rooms," Hannah continues.

Sienna looks surprised. "Oh, I think there's some confusion. I booked one of the smaller rooms."

Hannah looks down at the tablet in her hands and frowns. "I see a booking for Monroe & Carter for the grand ballroom on December 23rd."

"I think there's a mistake," Sienna insists. "The grand ballroom is completely out of our price range."

Hannah winces. "Let me get my manager." She pulls out her phone and steps away from us.

"I'm sure it's fine," Mom says, rubbing soothing circles on Sienna's back. My sister gives her a strained smile.

"It's probably because they have so many bookings," Sadie says. "Didn't you get your booking at the last minute?"

Sienna nods in agreement. This is where she wanted to get married because a lot of Luke's family is from Alberta and because our maternal side of the family lives here. Our grandmother, aunts and cousins will all be driving in from Vancouver in a couple of days. The event spaces here are booked out a year in advance and Sienna only managed to get it on the day there was a cancellation.

"My manager is on her way," Hannah explains. "Why don't we see the grand ballroom, anyway? I can show you the other rooms also."

"I don't want to see the grand ballroom and fall in love with it, only to have to move to another room," Sienna says.

Hannah smiles softly. "I understand. Let me assure you, the only thing grand about the grand ballroom is the size. All our ballrooms have similar views and you're going to get the same experience. Or you can wait in the restaurant."

"We'll wait in the restaurant," I say.

Hannah leads us to the restaurant that's empty at this time of the day. Apparently, they're only open for the dinner service starting at five. The bartender is already there setting up for the night as we walk in.

"Would you like something to drink?" Hannah asks.

"Water is fine," Dad says.

"Are you sure? It's on the house. We're really so sorry for the confusion."

"Don't worry about it, I'm sure we can get it sorted in no time," Sienna says.

I'm not so sure about that. How do you make a mistake like that when you're booking events every day? The good thing is they haven't charged us more than the deposit on the smaller ballrooms. I can't help thinking that if this is fucked up then everything else is going to be fucked up, too. That's just how my brain works. If one thing goes wrong, then everything goes wrong.

I take the glass of water the bartender sets on the counter, and something catches my eye in the mirror behind him. I turn and look at the wall behind me. There's a framed hockey jersey hanging on the wall. Three of them, actually. Number fourteen Hayes.

My blood turns to ice.

"Your owner is a big hockey fan?" Dad asks. "Or maybe a fan of the New York Renegades?"

Hannah follows Dad's gaze and laughs lightly. "Oh, those are his jerseys. Mr. Hayes Senior put them up years ago because he wanted to celebrate his grandson, but now he's the owner.

"No way! Connor Hayes is the owner of Cedar Creek Ranch?" Dad asks, excitedly.

"He is!" Hannah says, just as excited. "Oh, there they are now."

Hannah looks out the terrace windows and I see a man and woman walking across the snow-covered garden towards the restaurant. The man is wearing dark wash jeans, boots, a plaid jacket, and a black cowboy hat. Each step is confident and self-assured.

As if he can sense me looking, he looks away from the woman next to him and directly at me. Something tugs at the pit of my stomach, my heart slamming against the wall of my chest.

No, no, no. Fuck, no.

When he enters the restaurant, it's like all the air gets sucked out of the room and I suddenly can't breathe. Reaching up, he removes his hat, revealing his dark brown hair which has a smattering of grey now, just like his light beard.

His brown-ish green eyes rake over me and it's like my body comes alive. Like I'm coming in from the cold into a warm house that's been waiting for me. He comes to a stop in front of me, eyes soft, one corner of his mouth tilting up into a smile.

"Scarlett," he breathes.

The sound of his voice causes my body to erupt in goosebumps.

I don't know how I'm supposed to react right now or what he expects from me. My body cycles through emotions and the ones that stand out the most are hurt and anger.

So I do the only thing that will make me feel better.

I lift my hand and throw my water in Connor Hayes's face.

FOUR
CONNOR

"I love her," my best friend says quietly, next to me. The gleeful delight in her voice is unmistakable.

Scarlett watches me with angry blue eyes which tell me I should be thankful she didn't throw the glass at me with the water. Not that I don't deserve it. You don't break a woman's heart and then expect her to be fine with it because two years have passed.

Her family looks at us in shock.

"I wish I could say this is the first time she's done something like this," her mother mumbles.

She takes Scarlett's arm and pulls her back. Harvey holds out a towel for me and I take it from her, wiping away the water.

"Scarlett," I say again.

"Say my name one more time and I'm going to break this glass over your head," she hisses.

My little hellion.

"Angel," her father softly. I almost laugh, but I value my life too much. There's nothing angelic about this woman. She'll be sweet as sin until you do something to make her angry and then the hellion inside her comes out.

"I should step in before the police need to be called," Harvey says. "I'm Harvey, I'm the manager. I hear you're concerned about your booking?"

Scarlett's sister throws a curious look between the two of us before looking at Harvey. Scarlett continues to glare at me, but at least she's looking at me. At least she's not pretending I'm dead. That's a bonus in my book.

"I booked one of the smaller ballrooms for my wedding and I've just been informed by Hannah that we've been moved to the grand ballroom. That's out of our budget," her sister explains.

Harvey doesn't even blink. "I understand, the mistake was on our end. We accidentally booked you in the grand ballroom instead of one of the smaller ones. But don't worry, there will be no additional fees. We're also going to give you an open bar, at no additional cost to make up for our mistake."

Our sister blinks once, twice. Scarlett turns, her eyes narrowing on me. The lavender of her hair makes her eyes even paler and brighter.

The first time I saw her, two years ago, was when I was about to make a goal on the ice, and she was in the audience. Everything in hockey moves so fast I don't know how I saw her, but that lavender hair stood out against the crowd. And once I saw her, I couldn't look away. Everything seemed to stop. The noise of the crowd disappeared. My teammates, the game, the referee, coach, everything seemed to fall away.

There was just the woman behind the barrier, watching the game with curiosity. My heart pounded in my chest, my skin vibrating with an awareness I'd never experienced. Someone had slammed into me because I'd frozen solid on the ice, and I'd watched her laugh.

We lost the game and not even the disappointment from Coach and my teammates had been enough to dull the euphoric feeling. I'd rushed out of the dressing room to find her again because I knew, without a shadow of a doubt, I'd just met the love of my life.

It was like the universe knew this was my shot because I found Scarlett outside the arena. Her head was down as she texted on her phone and she looked up when I walked up to her, blue eyes widening in surprise, shoulder straightening as she got ready to defend herself.

I stopped a few feet away. "I'm Connor Hayes, captain of the Renegades. Do you want to grab a drink?"

"I'm on a date," she'd said, blinking in surprise.

"Any man who leaves you standing on the side of the road doesn't deserve you."

Scarlett's lips had tilted up into a curious smile. They were colored a deep red, in sharp contrast to the lightness of her hair and eyes. For a second, I almost thought I was hallucinating. That she was some fairy creature I'd conjured because I was suffering from too many traumas to the head.

"And what makes you so special, Connor Hayes? You're the captain of a team that just lost the game," she'd said.

"I was distracted."

She crossed her arms, a dark eyebrow arched in question. "By what?"

"By you. How is anyone expected to go on with his life when he's seen you? You're like an ethereal fairy princess. I'm afraid if I let you walk away now, I'll never find you again."

Surprise had flickered in Scarlett's eyes. Her date wandered up to us, stopping in the middle of what he was about to say when he saw me. She must have realized I was serious because Scarlett told him that was the end of their date, and she agreed to have a drink with me.

And now she can't even look at me. I have my work cut out for me.

It's been five hundred and thirty days, six hours and twelve minutes since I last saw her and every day has been a unique kind of torture. I didn't know love could feel this way.

Harvey suggests they see the grand ballroom and they all turn to walk away.

"Scarlett," I say again.

"I'll take this," one of her sisters says, taking the glass out of Scarlett's hand.

"She can hit me, I wouldn't mind."

"Thank you, Connor. Your permission is exactly what I was waiting for," Scarlett says, each word dripping with sarcasm.

"I can admit when I'm wrong," I say.

Scarlett's gaze turns icy. "Do you want a round of applause? Too bad there's no Stanley Cup for admitting you've fucked up. Then again, if there was a Stanley Cup, you wouldn't win it."

Behind her, her father winces. I grin at Scarlett. Not even the reminder that the Renegades lost the Stanley Cup the last year I played with them is going to dull the shine of this moment. Scarlett is here and she's talking to me. Her words might carry a sharp bite, but again, she's not pretending I'm dead. Progress.

"Let's go see the grand ballroom," her sister says, tugging on Scarlett's arm.

"Not if he's going," Scarlett says.

"He has other things to do," Harvey says. "It will be just us."

Harvey's brown eyes meet mine and the message in them is

clear. I need to give Scarlett space right now if I have any hope of winning her back.

Watching Scarlett walk away isn't easy. I left her once and I'm sure as fuck not going to make that mistake twice. She might hate me now, but I have two weeks to make her fall in love with me again.

FIVE
SCARLETT

Connor Fucking Hayes.

The last man I ever wanted to see again and now my sister is getting married in his lodge on his property. I don't believe for a second it was an innocent mistake that Sienna's booking was changed from the small ballroom to the grand ballroom without any additional fees and we were getting an open bar at no additional cost.

Thankfully, we don't see Connor again after Harvey gives us a tour of the lodge. The grand ballroom is as gorgeous as we expect it to be with sweeping arches, a breathtaking view of the Rockies, and a ten feet tall Christmas tree which Harvey says we can remove if we want.

Apparently, Silverpine takes their Christmas decorations very seriously.

As Sienna expected, she falls in love with the grand ballroom and takes out her phone to video call Luke.

"Scarlett, what was that?" Mom questions, while Sienna is busy showing Luke the view.

"What was what?" I ask.

"That," Mom motions towards the ballroom exit. "With Connor Hayes."

"Oh, that," I laugh, and it sounds fake and brittle to my own ears. "It was nothing."

I'm aware of Harvey standing close to us and even though her eyes are trained on her phone, I have no doubt her ears are open and listening to our conversation.

"Scarlett," Dad says. "That outburst was unexpected even from you. How do you know Connor Hayes?"

My throat closes up. How can I tell my parents and sisters that I dated someone for six months and hid it from them? How can I tell them now that he broke my heart and I barely survived because I loved him with every molecule of my being and seeing him now was a stab through my barely healed heart?

"Can we talk about this later?" I ask, glancing at Harvey.

Dad and Mom exchange a concerned glance. "Sure, Angel," Dad concedes.

Sadie puts her arm through mine as Mom and Dad turn to speak with Harvey.

"Is Connor the guy?" Sadie asks, her voice low. "The one who broke your heart?"

I sigh. I don't think it was easy to hide my heartbreak from my parents. It was even harder to hide it from my sisters. Mostly because we live together, and they saw me not leave the bed for weeks and avoid all mention of anything romantic.

"Yeah, that's him."

"You didn't tell us he was hot! Or that it's literally Connor Hayes!" Sadie says. "I hate him, obviously. But damn." She looks over our shoulders towards the ballroom entrance, trying to catch a glimpse of Connor. Not that he's anywhere to be seen.

I giggle despite myself. If there's anyone who can make me

laugh about this situation, it's my sisters. Connor still being as hot as ever makes this whole situation worse.

"I don't want to talk about him," I say.

Sadie snorts. "Too late for that now. You know mom and dad are going to want all the details."

"I didn't know he'd be here!" I protest. "He should have to explain what he did instead of me having to explain his indiscretions."

Sadie's eyes are sharp with anger when they meet mine. "Wait. Did he cheat on you? Because I've heard enough horror stories about dating hockey players."

"No, he didn't cheat on me."

I never doubted for a second that Connor was in love with me. I never worried that he was going to find someone more interesting, someone funnier or prettier. When he looked at me, I knew I was the only one he wanted, and he told me that every day.

He sent me flowers the night after we met with a card that said I should call him when I was ready, and he hoped I did because he wanted to see me again. I didn't call him for a week because I'd been love bombed before and he was older and more experienced. What the hell did he want with me? But the excitement in his voice was like a kid waking up to all his favorite toys on Christmas morning.

The intensity of being wanted by Connor Hayes was scary and wonderful. It was a heady experience that I never wanted to recover from.

"What did he do?" Sadie asks. "I'm going to hate him regardless, but I'd like to channel my anger productively."

I snort at her phrasing. When my parents put me into therapy, they thought it would be a good idea to send my sisters as well. It seemed to work for them better than it did for me. It's not the therapist's fault when the universe wants to continuously prove I'm right. I have an inkling and I'm rarely wrong.

"He left, Sadie," I say. "One day he was just gone. No phone call, no text. I went to his apartment, and he'd left a fucking letter with the doorman."

"What did the letter say?"

Opening my purse, I grab the letter from the back pocket and hold it out for her. Sadie's mouth drops open.

"Scarlett! You never read it?"

"What would be the point?" I put the letter back. "Sadie, he left. Anything he had to say, he could have said over a phone call or text. He never tried to get in touch with me, not even to check if I got the letter or if I read it. That tells me whatever is in the letter isn't that important."

Sadie frowns, but doesn't say anything. Truth is, I couldn't bring myself to read the letter those first few months. I knew whatever was in it was just going to make my heart hurt worse. After that, it didn't make much sense to revisit it.

"You obviously still care, otherwise you wouldn't be carrying it around with you," Sadie says.

Ugh, sisters.

"I thought you hate Connor?" I arch an eyebrow at her.

"I do," she agrees, widening her hazel eyes. "I also want to know what's in that love letter he wrote you."

"It's not a love letter," I say with a laugh. How can it be a love letter when he used it to dump me?

"What love letter?" Mom asks, turning to us.

"The one that Connor wrote to her, and she never read because she was rightfully angry he left without saying goodbye," Sadie says.

Mom gasps and I elbow Sadie lightly in the side. I held onto this heartbreak for a year and a half, and she revealed it in less than a second. Dad, Sienna, and Harvey are talking in the distance and thankfully haven't heard.

I grab mom's hand. "Please, let's not talk about this. I don't want it to overshadow Sienna's wedding, please."

Mom pinched her lips together and nodded. I can tell she wants to know more but she also knows I'm right. We're here for Sienna and should be focusing on her wedding going smoothly. We'll have family descending on us soon and we need to get everything in order.

"We'll talk about this when we get home," Mom says.

"Yes, absolutely. I'm all for it. I love talking about my feelings."

Both Mom and Sadie laugh at that. The last thing I want or enjoy is talking about my feelings. I've always been a little lost in my own world, getting irritated quickly and getting over it even quicker. I keep the hurt and the frustrations to myself, unlike the rest of my family who just love talking about their feelings.

Maybe it's because I'm the middle child and I always had emotions flowing over me through my sisters. There was always something happening that needed attention with them and I realized I hated any kind of attention so I just kept things to myself.

"Okay, we're going for lunch after this. Harvey was just telling us about a Christmas market and I thought we could do that this evening?" Mom says.

"Sounds fun!" I agree, forcing all the cheer I didn't feel into my words.

Sienna and Harvey exchange numbers in case anything goes wrong with the booking. I take a chance to really look at Harvey. She's gorgeous, tall and statuesque, the kind of woman I thought Connor would prefer. Her eyeliner is perfect, the wing sharp, hair pulled back into a ponytail with some strands left to frame her face.

I love her immediately. She has the kind of vibe that makes me feel comfortable, that invites me to open up and be her friend. I see it for the danger it is. I can't open up to her if she's Connor's friend.

As we're walking out of the lodge, she looks at me and grins.

I stop, letting my family go in front of me. "There wasn't a mix up with the booking, was there?"

Harvey shrugs innocently. "I'm not at liberty to say."

"I don't know what he thinks he's doing but my sister's wedding is very important to me and if he does anything to mess it up, he's going to regret it," I say.

Harvey nods once. "I'll pass that along to him."

I open my mouth to say more but my words get stuck in my throat when Connor walks out the door behind the reception desk. He's been running his hands through his hair because it's that perfect, floppy mess. I hate that I still remember what it felt like to run my hands through his hair.

He freezes when he sees me and for a second, we're locked in a stare-off. Looking at him makes my heart hurt, like someone has reached inside my chest and wrapped their hand around it.

He moves forward, opening his mouth.

I look away from him to Harvey. "Thank you for your help."

And then I walk away without another word, just like he did.

SIX
CONNOR

"She hates you, Connor," Harvey says, as we watch Scarlett walk out of the lodge.

"I wouldn't have guessed by the way she refuses to talk to me," I say. Something tugs inside my chest seeing Scarlett walk away. Some vicious part of me wants to kidnap her and lock her away until she forgives me.

"No, she, like, *really* hates you," Harvey says. Her dark eyes look gleeful.

"Are you sure you're my best friend, and not my worst enemy?" I raise an eyebrow at Harvey.

"No, that would be your brothers."

Harvey turns and walks towards her office. I have other things to worry about than my brothers right now, but I also can't let them do whatever they want because they're either going to get themselves killed or get someone else killed.

"Tell me honestly, should I move on?"

I'm thirty-eight years old and the head of this fucked up family since my grandfather died. Scarlett was eleven years younger, and those eleven years felt like a chasm between us now like they never did before.

I sit down in the visitor's chair across from Harvey's desk and run a hand through my hair. I've regretted every day I've been back. Not only leaving Scarlett but also coming back here as my grandfather requested and taking over this family.

"Trying to get your brothers to act like humans?" Harvey asks. "Yes, that's a lost cause. You're better off focusing on yourself."

"I meant, with Scarlett. Should I move on?"

Harvey stops and looks at me. "Do you want to move on? You've been trying for the last year and a half without any success."

I want Scarlett back in my life where she belongs. I knew the moment I looked at her that she was it for me. You don't meet someone like her and think you can do better because there is no one better. Her loyalty, her integrity, the way she loves with every part of her being. I'm never going to find that again and I don't want to.

"I want her back."

"Good," Harvey says. "Then you should know that she hates you. She also hasn't opened the letter you left her. And her family is going to the Christmas market tonight."

I wish I could say I'm surprised or disappointed Scarlett didn't read the letter.

I'm not.

I know my Scarlett a lot better than that. She keeps her emotions locked in a vault and I broke her heart. I'm not saying I'm not wrong and her anger isn't justified. If I was in her position, I wouldn't forgive me. I'm hoping that she will give me the grace to tell her that I love her even if she doesn't forgive me.

"Why are you so excited that she hates me?"

Harvey rests her chin on her upturned hand. "Because it's

annoying being friends with Connor Hayes, hometown hero. Everybody loves Connor Hayes. Connor Hayes can do no wrong."

She wrinkles her nose in distaste.

"It's not like I asked for it."

"But you do enjoy it," Harvey says.

I used to enjoy it. I never asked to be Connor Hayes, hometown hero, and I never asked to come back. I thought I would retire, Scarlett and I would move in together, maybe get married, and I'll never have to see Silverpine or Cedar Creek Ranch again. Until my grandfather got sick and demanded I come back.

If there was anyone I owed my loyalty to in this town, it was my grandfather. He wasn't an easy person to deal with, but he raised my brothers and me after our parents died. He left Cedar Creek to me because I'm the oldest and my brothers can't even be trusted to look after themselves.

If that wasn't enough, he made me the executor of both my brothers trust funds. I had to stay here and make sure they were on the straight and narrow if they wanted to see even a penny.

I'm an idiot for thinking Scarlett will want any part of this. She's twenty-seven, for fuck's sake. When I was twenty-seven, I'd just been traded to the New York Renegades and in my mind that meant a whole new city of women to experience.

I didn't want to settle down, definitely not in Silverpine of all places.

"Okay, new plan--"

Harvey groans. "Not another new plan, Connor. Let the woman decide what she wants. You've said it yourself, Scarlett is headstrong and always goes after what she wants regardless of what people think or say. What makes you think your plans are going to work, even if you know her well?"

"Stop trying to derail my plans before they even happen," I grumble.

"Stop making up ridiculous plans and just talk to her," Harvey fires back.

"She threatened to break glass over my head," I remind her.

Harvey scoffs. "Don't tell me you didn't thoroughly enjoy that."

"Of course, I did. She's like a fierce warrior princess right out of a fantasy novel."

That makes Harvey laugh. "If she takes you back, you're going to be insufferable."

It's the biggest *if* of my life.

SEVEN
SCARLETT

I'm not a self-conscious person, but I can't stop feeling like everyone is looking at me. It's an odd prickling on the back of my neck and when I turn to follow it, there's no one there.

I'm inclined to think that I'm being stalked. And the only person who would stalk me is Connor, though I don't think he'd take his life into his hand like that. No, it's the town people who are giving me strange looks the whole afternoon. I almost feel like I'm the part of a joke I'm missing or don't understand.

I stand up from the table I'm sitting at and walk up to the counter again to check on our food. After we visited Cedar Creek Ranch, we walked around the town, but Mom was too exhausted for the Christmas market. We decided to call it an early night and while the rest of my family went back to the Inn, I stopped in to pick up our dinner. Dad wanted to stay with me, but I sent him back as well. The Inn is only a five-minute walk away.

"Excuse me, I just wanted to check on my order, for Monroe. I've been waiting for over an hour," I say to the server behind the counter.

"It will be another few minutes. We're just very busy," she says, without looking up at me. I didn't doubt they were busy because we'd seen a bus full of tourists arrive earlier in the afternoon. But people who came after me had already picked up their order, so I found it a bit suspicious that mine was still not ready.

"Can you please check?" I ask in a voice that I hate to use. Sienna calls it my 'dealing with a bully voice'. It's hard and leaves no room for an argument.

The girl finally looks up and heaves a sigh. "Sure. Let me just drop everything and check."

Okay, something weird was definitely going on. All I'd ask her to do was her job. Maybe I caught her on an off day and maybe it was my fault for pushing her to check on my order. I will make sure to leave her a big tip.

The door behind me opens and I step aside to let the new person come in. Heat spreads across my back and when I breathe in, I'm hit with the clean, cool scent of winter and something warm and woodsy like sandalwood.

I stiffen, looking over my shoulder. My eyes meet dark green ones. Of course, it's Connor because the universe hates me and seems to have a personal vendetta against me. For a second, I consider leaving the food that's never going to be ready and walking out of here.

But why do I have to leave when I haven't done anything, and he gets to exist like he's the king of the world?

I turn around and face the counter, completely ignoring him. Which is hard to do when the man is 6'5" and he still makes my body hum like I'm coming alive. I feel him step up to the counter and I pull out my ereader to read the book I've auditioned for. Gemma St. James is one of my favorite authors and I've already recorded two books by her, but I definitely want this one. The main character is a little edgier, a lot unlikable, and a part of me really connects with her.

"Oh, Connor!" The server is back. "Your order will be ready in another minute or so."

She smiles at him sweetly and I feel that familiar hum of frustration and jealousy. I tamp down the latter emotion because I have no business being jealous over Connor.

"Thank you, Anna." God, the sound of his voice. It's rough and unexpectedly smooth, like a blend of whisky that's been aged to perfection and hits all the right notes.

"Can I get you something to drink while you're waiting?" Her cheeks flush pink and I get it. I've been there, specifically

I might as well be invisible to her, even with my bright lavender hair.

"Excuse me, what about my order?"

She frowns, looking at me like she's forgotten why I'm here. "Oh, uh, it's going to be another few minutes."

Either they were really, *really* busy, or something fishy was going on.

I feel Connor look at me as I try to control my anger. I have never in my life been rude to service workers because I might be an angry person but I'm not a shit person. I've worked in the service industry, and these are my people. So, my only choice here is to walk away and leave the order. Right? Because I can't be fucking angry at her that my order has taken over an hour to prepare.

"How long have you been waiting?" The question comes from Connor.

"Not long," Anna says. "We're very busy."

Connor is still looking at me and I wish he'll stop. Why is he making this more difficult than it needs to be? Something brushes against the edge of my coat, and I look down to see

Connor's hand flexing towards me before he clenches it into a fist.

I look up at him. He's looking at me plaintively, almost desperately. My heart squeezes painfully. I told myself I won't talk to him and I'm about to break that rule because I'm exhausted and he's here. I'm suddenly remembering how considerate he always was, always wanting me to be comfortable and safe. So protective.

I didn't need anyone to protect me, but I couldn't deny that it was nice to be protected. To have someone go to bat for me, or stand behind me ready to jump in.

"Over an hour," I say with a swallow.

Connor's jaw flexes as he grinds his teeth. "Wait here."

He turns and walks towards the back of the restaurant. The server glares at me and I don't understand what I've done wrong.

A minute later, Connor is striding back out with two paper bags in his hands. My stomach practically growls.

"I've got your order. Are you going back to The Honeysuckle?"

I can only nod. How does he know where I'm staying?

"I'll walk with you," he says.

"I have to pay," I protest.

"No, you don't," Connor said, simply. "You're getting free food here for the rest of your life if you want."

I...what? He shifts both food bags to one arm as he pushes open the restaurant door and waits for me to exit. I step out into the cold night and shiver, shoving my hands into the pocket of my coat.

I can hear people singing Christmas carols somewhere down the street. There's a group of people gathered around them, listening to the carolers. Connor gestures for me to cross the street so we don't run into them.

"You don't have to do this," I say. "I can carry the bag myself."

Being away from the restaurant is helping clear my head.

Connor glances at me through narrowed eyes. "I'm going to The Honeysuckle as well."

Why is he going to The Honeysuckle?

"This isn't going to fix anything, Connor. You can't do one nice thing and expect everything to be better."

His beautiful mouth lifts into a smirk.

"Baby girl, if I thought getting you back was going to be this easy, I wouldn't try because it'd mean I don't know you at all."

His words cause me to trip over my own feet. Connor reaches out and wraps his arm around my waist, steadying me. My body is flush against his and for a second, I'm taken back to all those times he'd pulled me close and kissed me just because. He'd always say that. We'd be walking down the street, and he'd pull me close to kiss me *just because* with this secretive smile on his face.

His face is so close to mine, the feel of his body so familiar. His eyes look brown right now, thickly lashed, his nose straight, lips soft and inviting. He hasn't shaved in at least a week and there's grey coming through his beard now. I always found that so hot.

There's a part of me that hates me for wanting to give in and ease my body against his. It's the part of me which enjoys going home to my parents' apartment where I grew up and settling into my old, comfortable places. Places where I always know I'll be safe.

I shove away from Connor. He's not a safe space anymore.

"There's no winning me back, Connor," I grind out. "This isn't a game."

He stares back at me with conviction. "Never thought it was, baby girl." His eyes flicker down my body in a slow perusal, my body flushes with heat. "And these aren't the games I want to play with you."

"Don't call me that," I say through gritted teeth. "Don't look at me like that either. Have you ever considered that I might have a boyfriend, and I've moved on from a man who left me without a second thought?"

I always hated when he called me that nickname, even though I missed hearing it. Connor looks at me for a long moment, tilting his head. I shiver as the wind picks up, carrying with it the scent of nutmeg and cinnamon from the bakery nearby.

"Then tell me you have a boyfriend, hellion," he says.

Ugh. I don't have the patience to deal with him. I turn and start walking towards the Inn again, letting him trail behind me. I hated liars and I didn't like lying so I'm not going to tell him that I'm seeing someone, not even to get him to back off. I'll be gone in two weeks, regardless.

"That's what I thought," Connor says, coming up beside me. "For the record, even if you had a boyfriend, I would do everything in my power to get you back because I know you belong with me."

I turn to glare at him. "Thank you for showing respect for my autonomy, Connor. I can always rely on you to be considerate."

Something flickers in his eyes, and I know I've hit him where it hurts. But then he smiles.

"I deserve that," he concedes. "I suppose when we were together you never got to see how desperate I am for you. I was able to hide it better. I can't do that anymore. So, yes, baby girl, even if it makes me a villain, I would have done everything to get you back."

I swallow thickly. When we were together, he would video call me every day he was gone for an away game and we would talk for hours. When he was in the city, he would demand we spend every minute together, keeping me in bed, fucking me slow and sweet, hard and dirty, until I forgot everything else. When he looked at me, I knew he saw nothing else.

If *that* was him hiding it, what will he be like if he doesn't hide it?

A group of old men walk out of a diner and their eyes alight on Connor. They're probably all in their seventies or there about.

"Connor! What do you think of the Knight's decision to trade Nolan?" One of them asks.

"They were treating him terribly. It's the best decision for Nolan. He's just a kid," Connor says.

"But they were playing well with him on the team. They had a chance to go to the playoffs," another said.

Connor laughs. "I'm sorry, but the Knights are never going to the playoffs. They have terrible plays, and they need a new coach."

It all sounded like gibberish to me. Despite dating a hockey player, I'd never developed any interest in the game. Not that Connor ever cared. He always patiently explained the game to me when I asked, even though I was sure my questions were repetitive.

Stop, stop, stop. This is a terrible way to stay single. Don't give in!

"Did you take Midnight out for a ride this morning? Thought I saw you out there," one of the men says.

"Yeah, he likes it when it's quiet and there's no one around," Connor says.

I glance at him in question. I assume Midnight is a horse, a black horse given the name. I was racing against a black horse this morning.

"Have a good night, fellas. Don't get into too much trouble,"

Connor says to them. He places a hand on my back and gently urges me forward. I wave at the old men. Before I can tell him to do so, Connor drops his hand back to his side.

"Was it you this morning?" I ask. "You were riding the horse."

My voice is accusatory.

Connor looks at me from the corner of his eye. "I was."

I didn't really need his confirmation because now that I think about it, it made sense it was Connor. I've always felt this intense connection to him, this pull deep inside me, like my molecules are calling out to him.

I breathe a sigh of relief when I see the Inn. Climbing up the steps, I push open the door and step into the warm lobby. Marion is behind the counter as always, humming along to the Christmas songs she's playing on an old radio. She looks up when we walk in and smiles brightly.

"Connor! I was wondering what was keeping you so long."

Is there someone he didn't know in this town? I know they always show people in small towns as knowing all their neighbors, but I didn't think that was actually true. Who has the time in this economy to know about their neighbors' lives? But Silverpine might as well be out of a movie.

"There was an issue at Patty's," Connor says.

"I see you ran into one of our guests," Marion says, looking at me. "Will I see you down here later with the rest of your family?"

"Later?" I question.

"We're having movie night," Marion explains. She motions behind her where the adjacent dining room has been turned into a mini theatre. All the couches and chairs have been moved to one side and lined in rows in front of a large TV.

"Every night in December, we watch Christmas movies. Connor sets it all up. I can't do technology," Marion adds. The latter part is obviously a lie because that morning she'd been texting on her phone faster than Sadie, and my sister is practically attached to her phone.

"That sounds fun," I say. I can't imagine anything worse than hanging out with a bunch of strangers. I love Christmas movies as much as the next girl, but this set up is my literal nightmare. "I should head back up to my family before they kill me for making them wait for dinner."

I hold out my hand for Connor to give me the bag of food.

"I can help you carry it up, it's heavy," he says.

"I'm not made of glass." I make a gimme gesture with my hand.

"But you're just as delicate."

"And just as sharp when broken."

I raise an eyebrow. With a grin, he puts the handle of the bag in my hand, letting his fingers graze over my palm. I hold back the shiver which threatens to erupt all over my body. Closing my fist over the handle, I lower my arm.

Connor holds my gaze. "See you later, baby girl."

I smile at him sweetly. "Maybe in your dreams, Connie."

His eyes narrow at me and Marion laughs lightly as I turn towards the stairs. Two can play at this game. If he wants to use a nickname I hate, then I'm going to use one he hates. And that's how we're going to spend the next two weeks.

EIGHT
SCARLETT

Christmas is my sister's favorite holiday, which is why she wanted to get married two days before Christmas so it will all be one big holiday. Her requirement was getting married where they celebrated Christmas to the max.

All of that explains the reason why I'm wearing matching pajamas with my family and sitting in the dining room of an Inn, about to watch *A Miracle on 34th Street.* Sienna is sitting next to me on the couch, the wedding bible open in front of her. I already have everything taken care of and I'm going to meet with the vendors to make sure everything will go smoothly on the big day.

"Given the size of the grand ballroom, I think we could have invited more people," Sienna says.

"I agree," Mom says from her other side. "We'll have to make some adjustments, otherwise the room is going to look mostly empty."

"How could we have invited more people when this was all a mistake?" I ask.

Sienna and Mom look at me, smiling at me with their eyes. "Was it a mistake?" Sienna asks casually.

Simultaneously, they turn and look at where Connor is talking with Marion and another guest. They seem to think this 'mistake' was Connor's doing. I'm not sure they're wrong, but I'm also not sure they're right. How would Connor have known my sister booked the event space in his family's lodge?

"Not that we know what kind of man he is since we've never met him before," Mom says pointedly.

I sigh, sliding deeper on the couch.

As soon as I'd walked into the room with our dinner earlier, they'd demanded to know everything about Connor and me. Their main question was why I hadn't told them about Connor even though we'd dated for six months.

"Because I couldn't figure out a way to introduce someone as my boyfriend," I'd said. "It's not like Luke, who came over for a group project in the ninth grade and never left."

"What's so hard about saying 'This is Connor, my boyfriend'?" Sadie had asked. "I've done it lots of times."

"I don't know," I'd said, shifting uncomfortably. I'd looked to dad for help because he's the only one who understands me. My sisters take after our mother, both outgoing and fun. I take after dad--if given the option, I prefer to stay at home and not socialize.

"I thought we agreed we're not going to talk about it until after the wedding?" Dad said.

Sienna paused in the middle of eating her salad. "But I need relationship tea. Is no one else offended that Scarlett didn't tell us about her relationship?"

"Scarlett isn't like you or your sister, Princess," Dad said. "She needs time with these things."

"She had almost two years," Mom said. "This man clearly

broke her heart and none of us knew a single thing. I find it very concerning."

I understand why she thinks it's concerning, but it really doesn't need to be. I love my family and it's not like I'm incapable of expressing emotions. I'm just a little more reserved in that department.

"When she's ready, she'll tell us about it," Dad said. It seemed to draw an end to that topic.

I know dad is upset I didn't tell anyone. But I don't know how to explain the sheer awkwardness I feel when I think of bringing someone home and introducing them to the family. It's not because my family is unpredictable or wild, or because I'm embarrassed of them. I find the whole idea of introducing someone to your family extremely cringe, for some reason. Like, *hi family, this is the person I'm currently having sex with.*

There's a reason my parents put me in therapy, okay.

"I know you don't want to hear it," Sienna says now, "but he does keep looking over here."

I didn't have to look up from my ereader to know that. Connor's gaze is heavy as it lands on me again and again, settling on me like a thousand butterflies.

"I wish I knew if I should encourage him or not," Mom says.

"Ma," I groan, lowering my ereader. "Just let it be."

"Okay, okay." Mom raises her hands in surrender. I know she's not one to drop it this easily, but dad and Sadie bring over our hot chocolates and that keeps her from asking more.

I shift to the loveseat next to the couch with Sadie, letting dad sit next to mom. Other than dad, Sadie is the only one who won't ask too many questions. We settle in and Sadie pulls a throw over us.

I have to admit, Marion has gone out of her way to make this cozy and comfortable and friendly. This is the kind of niche thing which makes people come back or tell their friends about it. There's a healthy turn out of guests, there's three different varieties of hot chocolate and many types of Christmas cookies. Music is playing softly from a speaker, and if all that isn't enough, snow begins to fall softly outside.

Marion turns off the music and steps up in front of the TV.

"Thank you so much for coming, everyone. Every year I do this, I think it's the year no one is going to show up, but I do it anyway." She looks around at the Christmas tree and decorations, sighing deeply.

"Christmas was my husband's favorite time of the year. He always went all out and there were always big parties at the ranch. This is the second year I'm doing it without him but I'm so grateful to have my grandson here to help an old woman." She smiles at Connor.

"Pretty sure you're going to outlive us all," he says.

"That's what we used to say about your grandfather," Marion says, making everyone laugh.

He helps her sit down in a large chair and turns the movie on, sitting down in the chair beside her. While everyone is focused on the movie, I use the cover of darkness to watch Connor. I used to wonder if I'll ever see him again and what I'll say to him if I do. Now here he is, talking to Marion in low whispers, laughing quietly at whatever she's saying.

"You're staring," Sadie whispers.

"I know," I whisper back.

Marion said this is the second year she's celebrating Christmas without her husband. Connor left New York in August of that same year, the news of his sudden retirement a shock. That must mean his grandfather died then, or shortly after. Connor told me his grandfather raised him and his brothers, but he'd never wanted to stay here so he'd fought with his grandfather to leave.

I don't want to know the reasons why he left New York because I want to hold on to my anger for as long as possible. But I can't stop myself from feeling a twinge of sympathy for the man I loved. I can't help wondering if he left because of a family emergency. But then why didn't he tell me? I would have gone with him, I would have supported him. I'm not fucking heartless.

Connor looks up and right at me, our eyes meeting in the darkness. From the moment he asked me out, I haven't been able to describe this pull I feel towards him. It's like my soul recognizes his soul and wants to be near him.

"Oh, this is *so* not over," Sadie mumbles next to me.

"Sadie!" I hiss.

"Don't say my name like that," she says. "I'm not the one making intense eye contact with my ex after throwing water in his face, threatening to break glass over his head, and telling my family I don't care about him."

I wince. I have been embarrassingly erratic today. I force myself to look away from Connor. It feels like pulling apart something that's been stuck with glue.

"It's over," I tell Sadie.

"Uh-huh." She nods, glancing between me and Connor. "I believe you."

"We're not getting back together," I say.

"Sure," Sadie says, sipping on her hot chocolate.

"I don't care what you say. I have to focus on the wedding."

"I believe you. I'm on your side."

It doesn't feel like she's on my side. It doesn't feel like I believe half the things I'm telling her.

NINE
SCARLETT

When I go running over the next few days, I skip Cedar Creek Ranch. Not that it helps because I see Connor around town all the time. He's helping someone carry a big box from the hardware store, or he's talking to the same group of old men, or he's helping Marion put up even more Christmas decorations.

One day, I come down and Marion is directing him to hang garlands over the staircase railing.

"It's like Santa's village of the damned in here," Connor says. "It's too much."

"It's never too much," Marion says, her eyes finding me. "What do you think, Scarlett?"

Connor looks up at me and I avoid his gaze. Mostly because I'm worried he'll be able to tell I've been thinking about him.

"You can never have too many Christmas decorations," I say, smiling at her. "Tis the season."

"Don't listen to her," Connor warns, continuing to decorate. "She hates Christmas."

"People change, Connie," I say sweetly.

Marion steps away to greet guests who've just arrived.

"Going out, baby girl?" Connor asks, his eyes dragging over me.

"Not that it's any of your business, but yes. I'm going out for a walk."

My family is in Calgary for the day while I was sleeping off a headache. I'm going stir crazy inside, so some fresh air is needed.

"Need some company?"

"Not yours," I say, on my way out.

I grab a pumpkin spice latte from the cafe across the street and just walk around town. It really is picturesque. The mountains are so close they loom over us, and I feel like if I walk in a straight line, I'll get to them.

There's a black truck with tinted windows I see driving around everywhere I turn, but it usually speeds up and drives past just when I start growing suspicious.

I try to keep my mind off Connor, but it's not easy when I keep running into him everywhere.

The day after I found him decorating the Inn, I'm in the bookstore and as I round the corner, who should I run into but Connor.

"Is stalking me part of your plan to get me back?" I ask.

"I can't lie and say I didn't consider it," he admits, mouth tilting up into a smirk.

"Stop trying to make us happen, Connie. It's never going to happen. You ghosted me six months into our relationship."

I slide the book I'm holding back on the shelf. I'm acutely aware that we're the only two people here other than the owner and they can probably hear our conversation even though our voices are low.

"Not because I wanted to," Connor says, brows drawn in. "I never *wanted* to leave, Scarlett."

"That doesn't make it better, Connor," I snap.

"I never said it did. I don't claim to be anything other than an absolute asshole for the way I ended things, but if I'd seen you..." he trails, swallowing thickly. "If I'd seen you I wouldn't have been able to leave and I was too fucked in the head to think of anything else."

A very small piece of me thaws, hearing the pain in his voice. I know now his grandfather died shortly after he left, but it doesn't make my heartbreak fickle. The only thing left to do is forgive him and try to move on, which I can't find myself doing right now.

"I have to go," I tell him.

IT'S BEEN a couple days since my talk with Connor in the bookstore and the only time I saw him in town was when he was helping people around town. I don't know how he has so many regulars, but this is Connor to the core.

I need to focus on my sister's wedding and making sure everything is ready for the big day instead of wondering about Connor.

Even dad is growing concerned.

"Do you want to talk about it?" Dad asks, on our drive back to the Inn this morning. I hate having him drive behind me, so I usually drive back with him after I've completed my run instead of running back.

I chew on the straw of my coffee and then spat it out when I remembered it's a paper straw.

"Connor is literally the last person I want to be thinking about right now," I tell him. "Sienna's getting married and I'm her maid of honor. She needs me to focus on her and what she wants."

"But you're thinking about Connor?" Dad asks, glancing at me.

"It's a disease. Even when he wasn't around I was thinking about him and now it's gotten worse and we've only been here for seven days."

Dad's the only one I can talk to about this because I know he won't get excited. He's definitely the kind of father who isn't happy when his daughters bring home a boyfriend.

"Do you want him back?" Dad asks.

"I never want to see his face again."

"Never?" Dad looks at me from the corner of his eye and smirks.

I sip my coffee. "He's nice to look at, but right now, that's about the only thing he's got going for him," I admit.

"What if he begs for your forgiveness and wants to get back together?"

Baby girl, if I thought getting you back was going to be this easy, I wouldn't try because it'd mean I don't know you at all.

Was he serious when he said it? Does Connor actually think there's even a chance we're going to get back together? This isn't a movie where everything is going to be magically resolved in two weeks. Besides, he lives here, and I live in New York. Clearly, the man thinks long distance relationships can't work otherwise he wouldn't have disappeared from my life.

"I don't know, Daddy," I say. "He'll have to get down on his hands and knees and beg like his life depended on it. Maybe then I'll consider forgiving him."

"Connor Hayes," Dad says quietly, with disbelief.

"Bet you didn't expect me to be the child who dated a professional athlete," I say, grinning.

Dad laughs, signaling right to turn into the parking lot for The Honeysuckle.

"You're the child I never expected to date," he says honestly.

"Yeah, that tracks."

I'm the kind of girl who never leaves the house and expects the love of her life to somehow find her. In my case, I didn't find him. He found me in a crowd of thousands of people, while he was in the middle of a game, and I was on a date with another man.

"Don't tell Mom I talked to you," I say, as dad parked the car.

"Angel, I've been married to your mother for thirty-four years. I know when not to tell her things."

I can't stop the snort-laugh which erupts out of me. I hold my cup out in front of me so I don't spill coffee everywhere.

"What's so funny?" Dad asks, giving me a weird look and a curious smile.

"Connor is thirty-eight. It's just weird to think that my ex-boyfriend is older than my parents' marriage."

Dad makes a horrified face which only made me laugh harder.

"Age is just a number," I say.

"And hell is just a sauna," he quotes, making me laugh harder.

THE NEXT DAY, while my sisters and mother go shopping, Dad stays back to take a nap, and I go make sure the wedding vendors are ready to have everything prepared on the Big Day. Which is only six days away.

My first stop is the Butter & Bloom, the bakery where we ordered the wedding cake. They're reportedly the best bakery in town and as soon as I step in, I can see why. It smells like cinnamon and nutmeg and fresh coffee. My stomach growls at the scent.

All varieties of baked goods are displayed behind the glass, and I'm drawn to their holiday flavors, which feature a cinnamon roll cake, vanilla cake with nutmeg ganache, gingerbread cupcakes, peppermint cupcakes, and more. My mouth practically waters.

I miss our shop. This is our busiest time of the year, but my parents have chosen a great manager for the shop and Niles runs a tight ship. During the holidays, we always have to hire extra help, and our chocolate pies have a waiting list that starts in the summer because there's only so many chocolate pies we can bake.

"Can I help you?" The teenage girl behind the counter asks.

"Can I get a peppermint mocha and an assortment of your holiday cupcakes? I also have a custom order for a wedding cake for next week and I want to check everything is fine with that."

"Sure thing! Let me take care of your order first and I'll get the manager," she says.

She rings up my order and passes it to me. I sit down at a table so I'm not holding up the line and sip my peppermint mocha. It's perfectly hot, which is what I like.

I look out the window and see a woman across the street with a little girl, both carrying bags from the local clothing store.

There's an ease to life here that I've never seen in New York. I'm not sure New Yorkers even know how to slow down. Here, everyone seems to know everyone, and this is where Connor grew up. The town he left because he couldn't stay here and be one of them.

"Excuse me?" I look up at a man about my age standing in

front of me. He's wearing an apron over his jeans and t-shirt, his hair disheveled. "You said you had a wedding cake you're picking up next week?"

"Yes! For the Monroe/Carter wedding on December 23," I say.

"Let me check," he says.

He walks behind the counter and types something on the cashier's screen. Whatever he sees makes him frown. He converses with the cashier, and she shrugs before walking into the kitchen. When she comes out, she whispers something to him, and he sighs before walking back over to me.

I don't have a good feeling about any of this, but I give him the benefit of doubt until he opens his mouth and speaks. "We don't have a booking for Monroe/Carter for December 23."

I blink at him. "Then I guess the booking confirmation I received must have been from another Butter & Bloom bakery in Silverpine. If you tell me where it is, I'll promptly make my way over there."

He shifts on his feet, his cheeks brightening with color. "There isn't another Butter & Bloom in Silverpine."

"Yeah, I figured as much," I say, with as much sarcasm as I can manage. "Then there must be a reservation in your system because there's definitely a deposit in your system and I'm not in the habit of spending money without getting some kind of proof. So, either give me back my deposit or bake the cake I hired you to bake."

He looks over his shoulder and I follow his gaze to a woman standing in the doorway to the kitchen. She gives me a hard look before disappearing inside.

"Who is that?" I ask.

"That's the owner."

"Can I talk to her about this missing reservation?" I ask.

I'm very proud of myself for not exploding right now.

Because the anger I'm feeling is simmering at the edge and I'm one push away from toppling over and spewing it at this innocent man.

"I don't think that's a good idea," he says.

"What's your name?"

He blinks at me owlishly. We have to be the same age, yet I can't help thinking he's afraid of me. Good. He should be very afraid because if something goes wrong with my sister's wedding then this whole town is going to remember my name, and not for good reasons.

"Shane."

"Shane, you seem reasonable enough, so let me explain to you clearly. My sister is getting married, which means we need a cake. The cake I ordered six months ago and for which I provided a deposit and for which I received a confirmation. If the cake is not going to be ready for us on December 23, exactly as I ordered it, then I'm going to become your worst nightmare."

I raise my eyebrows. "Are we on the same page?"

"Uh, I just work here," he says.

I pinch the bridge of my nose. I can't tell Sienna that she's not going to have a cake for her wedding. I'm the maid of honor, it's my responsibility to fix this mess for her. If I have to become an expert baker myself, then I'll do it.

"You've been no help at all, Shane."

I grab my drink and throw it in the trash on my way out the door.

Okay, don't panic. You've got this.

I take a few bracing breaths of the cold air which smells like sugar cookies and I'm no closer to calming down.

"Fuck!"

"Oh, dear."

I whirl around and see Marion standing beside me on the sidewalk with Harvey next to her. Today, Harvey's hair is in an intricate braid which is wrapped around her head like a crown. She's in a long black coat, a black scarf wrapped around her neck. Marion's short bob looks freshly blow dried and she's wearing a red coat and a white scarf with little reindeers on it.

"Sorry," I murmur.

"Is everything okay?" Harvey asks, glancing between me and the door of the bakery. Concern lines her face.

"These...*people* 'lost' the confirmation for my sister's wedding cake so now we don't have a cake. I sent them the deposit, I have an email confirmation, but *Shane* tells me there's nothing he can do, and I can't speak to the owner. I had to walk out of there before I flew into a rage."

Harvey and Marion exchange looks that, for all I know, means they're wondering how Connor ended up with someone like me. He's so calm, and sensible, and never overreacts.

"What is it?" I ask.

"I hoped something like this wouldn't happen," Marion says. "It's petty and extremely childish."

Harvey puts a hand on my back and ushers me across the street to the parking lot so we're not standing in the middle of the sidewalk.

"The Hayes family have a reputation in Silverpine," Harvey says. "There isn't a single person here who doesn't have a story for when a Hayes family member jumped in to help them when they desperately needed it. They have a goodwill."

My bones are icy, and it has nothing to do with the bitter wind. This tracks with what I've seen, with Connor helping people with the littlest of things.

"What does that have to do with me?" I ask quietly.

"What Harvest is trying to say is, people in the town hero worship my husband's family," Marion says. "Which means they often refuse to see when those boys are in the wrong and they're all too eager to support them in their wrongs."

Marion sighs. "Everyone knows Connor was heartbroken when he came back and that he hasn't been able to move on. In their minds, they've made you the villain."

I look down at the Butter & Bloom box in my hands, the flowery script and the swirls of the letters.

"In their minds, they don't have a shot with Connor because of you," Harvey adds. "It's fucked up, I know. It doesn't help that everyone thought Jane and Connor would end up together before Connor left for Toronto and never came back."

My phone chimes in my pocket and I pull it out to see a text from Sienna.

SIENNA

We're going out for lunch after shopping. Are you almost done? Mom got you a dress she thinks you'll like.

"I suppose there's no point going to the florist?" I look up just in time to see Marion and Harvey exchange glances. Right.

On the outside, this town might look like a Hallmark movie, but deep down it's a horror movie filled with characters who hate me for something I haven't done. Does Connor know what's happening here? Is that why my dinner took over an hour to prepare last night?

Oh, these people.

I want to get back together with Connor just so these people can't have him, and I actually want to dump him this time because if I'm going to be villainized, I actually want to do the crime.

"Thank you for all that information," I say. "Harvey, are you going back to the lodge?"

"It's my day off but I don't want to miss whatever this is," she says almost gleefully.

"Darn, I have to go back to the Inn," Marion says.

"I'll record it for you."

"I don't know what's happening," I say.

Harvey rolls her eyes. "Nobody ever gets angry at Connor because he's the NHL star. The hometown hero who can do no wrong."

"I'm surprised he's not a raging narcissist," I say.

"I know! He's nice, which makes it worse."

I look at Marion. "I'm sorry, I know he's your grandson, but he's also the most hated man in my world."

"He did the crime, he can do the time. Give him hell," she says.

I text Sienna to let her know that I won't be joining them for lunch. I have some things to take care of.

TEN
CONNOR

"The fence on the east side of the property is down again and the cows have been trying to make a break for it."

I look up at my ranch foreman, Oliver, when he steps into the den in the back of the house. My grandfather used it as his office, and this is where he did all his business. It was an unnecessary addition to the house as far as I'm concerned because its three walls are covered in large windows overlooking the west side of the property. Which means in the winter, this room is cold as ice no matter how warm the rest of the house is.

"I thought Cage was supposed to fix that," I say.

Oliver sits down in the chair across from me, running a hand through his blonde hair. He's the same age as me, came into town five years ago and got hired by my grandfather on the spot. It still bothers me that I don't know his background, I don't know if he's ever worked on a ranch, or if he's hiding a criminal past we just don't know about.

"Nope. I haven't seen Cage in two days. His baby mama called, and he disappeared faster than a needle in a haystack," Oliver says.

"This is the third time he's done this in a month," I say.

"Your grandfather never had any problems with him," Oliver says, in a tone which could mean I'm the idiot or my grandfather was losing his mind.

"Let's go," I say.

We fix up the fence and make sure the cows are not escaping. It's bitter cold and I help Oliver inspect the cows for sickness and injury before doing the same with the horses.

"You're really going to open the lodge again?" Oliver asks, as we're cleaning the stables.

"Yeah. The plans are drawn up and work will start in the summer."

Because the lodge and the ranch are on the same property, I had plans drawn up to separate the two so I can keep people away from this side of the property.

"People like seeing the horses," Oliver says. "They don't get that in their real lives."

"We'll get the horses to the lodge, Oliver."

"Will you keep the people away from here?"

I straighten from scrubbing the floor and give him a flat look. "Oliver, no one is coming here who I don't want."

As I say it, there's a rumbling of a car coming up the driveway. It agitates the horses, and they start to whine. Oliver calms them, looking at me in question.

"You were saying?"

"You work for me, remember?" I remind him.

I pass him the broom on my way out of the stable. There's a black car coming up the driveway to the house. I pull off my work gloves and start walking back. I'm not expecting any visitors, and no one really comes to this part of the ranch. Since it's just me here, I haven't bothered with Christmas decorations either.

The car stops and I see a dark-haired man get out. He walks

around the front and opens the passenger door for a red-haired woman and laughs at something she says. The laugh takes me by surprise because for as long as I've known him, I've never seen Roman Maddox laugh or even smile. Love does strange things to a man.

Roman and I played for the Renegades together until he was traded to New Jersey. He plays for the Boston Titans now and got married last year, a fact which made me laugh when he told me. I thought he was joking.

He looks up when I get closer and smiles. "Were you out milking the cows?"

"I was fixing the fence and then helping clean the stables, asshole. The cows were milked in the morning."

"Watch the foul language in front of my wife," he says. The redhead next to him throws him a funny look.

"Babe, I've been surrounded by athletes my whole life. I've heard far worse." She turns to me, her eyes bright green. "We didn't mean to drop by unannounced. Roman thought it would be fine."

"Of course, he did."

"What are friends for?" Roman shrugs.

"This from a man who refused to admit we were friends for years," I tell his wife.

Roman rolls his eyes. "I wanted Lavinia to meet you. She needed confirmation that I had friends before she came into my life."

"I always knew you had friends," Lavinia says. "It's so nice to meet you," she says to me. "I'm a big fan."

Roman wraps his arm around her waist and pulls her toward him. "She's just saying that, she doesn't actually mean it."

"Roman!" Lavinia chides, laughing. "He's going to send us

back before he even invites us into the house if you keep up like that."

"You're allowed here anytime," I tell her. "Him, I'm not too sure about."

I lead them toward the front porch and up the steps to the house. "Would you like a cup of coffee?"

"Lavinia won't be coming back without me," Roman says. "Isn't that right, Blossom?"

Lavinia smiles up at him sweetly. "I don't know. It's a stunning view."

Roman smirks, leaning down to whisper something in her ear. Jealousy stabs me as I look away and make my way to the kitchen. I had what they have, and I fucked it all up. I was still fucking it up. I left because I thought Scarlett would be better off without me, better off without the family drama that she definitely didn't sign up for. I'm paying for making that decision for her.

"You have a beautiful home," Lavinia says, as they enter the kitchen. "It must be so amazing waking up to that view."

"It is," I agree, looking out the windows at the mountains behind the house. "Except when it gets dark at five, there's no one around and every sound makes you jump."

"Are you afraid of the dark, Connor?" Roman asks with a smile.

"Yeah, I'm a sensible man and I can admit that there are more things out there than scientists have discovered so far."

I make them both coffee and offer to make lunch, which they decline. So, I suggest we go into town for lunch. They're only here for the day and then driving back to Whistler where they are meeting Lavinia's brother and best friend.

Going into town will give me an opportunity to see Scarlett. It's as I'm thinking this that the front door opens and her voice rings out.

"Connor Fitzgerald Hayes!"

"Your middle name is *Fitzgerald?*" Roman can barely control his laugh.

"It's actually Frederick," I mumble, distracted. I set down my coffee cup and round the counter, walking out of the kitchen. The kitchen is directly across from the entrance, and I see Scarlett as soon as I walk out.

Her violet hair is wild and windswept, lips berry red, and she's looking at me like I'm the enemy of the state. Harvey stands next to her with a little smile on her face that I know doesn't bode well for me. She's holding a bakery box that I recognize is from Butter & Bloom.

"*You,*" Scarlett hisses. She stalks across the foyer, her heels clicking on the tiled floor. "It's because of you that my sister's wedding is going to be ruined! This whole town is in love with you and now they're cancelling our wedding orders because apparently, I'm some kind of villain who broke your precious little heart."

Scarlett huffs, shoving a piece of hair out of her face, her eyes burning at me furiously.

"Listen to me very carefully, Connor. I don't care what you have going on for the next week. Unless it's a life or death emergency, your time is mine. You're going to help me find a new baker and a new florist and a new spa and I don't care what you do to make them fit us in at the last minute. *Nothing* is going to ruin my sister's wedding. This is happening because of you and you're going to fix it!"

She shoves a finger against my chest. "I'm not kidding and I'm not going to let you off the hook for this. If a single thing goes awry, I'm going to haunt you for the rest of your life, and the rest of your afterlife, too." She leans closer, hissing up at me. "Don't have any doubts."

God, how I love this woman. I don't doubt her intentions to

haunt me, but in her anger, she probably doesn't realize it's exactly what I want.

"Do you promise?" I ask.

Scarlett narrows her eyes. "What?"

"Do you promise to haunt me for the rest of your life and the afterlife? Because I'll do anything you ask as long as you promise to haunt me."

Scarlett closes her eyes and takes a deep breath. I glance at Harvey, and she shakes her head in disappointment.

"I'm never going to be free of you," Scarlett murmurs. "Not even in the afterlife."

"Never, baby girl," I promise. "I'm afraid you sealed that deal when you told me you love me."

Opening her eyes, Scarlett looks at me. Behind all the hurt and anger, I still see glimmers of our love. Maybe they're just memories, maybe not. All I know is, if there's even a small chance, I'm taking it.

"And you said we should have stayed in Whistler," Roman says from behind me. "We would have missed this pure cinema."

Scarlett balances, looking behind me at Roman and Lavinia. "I didn't realize you were entertaining."

"He's not entertaining," Roman says. "In fact, he's more boring than I am. He lives on a farm in the middle of nowhere."

Scarlett cracks a smile, thawing a little. I glare at Roman. I'm the one who should be making her laugh and thawing the ice around her heart, not him. But when I look at him and then Scarlett, I realize she's seeing a man in love, so he's not a danger. Roman is standing next to Lavinia, an arm wrapped around her waist, and when he looks at her there's no doubt she's the only one who matters.

"It's a ranch, not a farm," I correct. "And I'm extremely entertaining."

Scarlett makes a sound that could be a laugh, and I turn to her in question. "Can we talk in private?"

"We can wait in the kitchen," Harvey says, walking further into the house.

"Don't eat all the cupcakes," Scarlett says to her. "I want to save some for Connor to choke on them later."

Harvey snickers as she, Lavinia, and Roman disappear back into the kitchen. I take Scarlett's arm and lead her into the living room.

"Why do you want me to choke on cupcakes, baby girl?"

Scarlett is looking around the living room, at all the photos my grandfather hung up. She stops in front of the wedding photo of my parents and looks back at me.

"Because you're ruining my sister's wedding, Connie."

I ignore the ridiculous nickname and step closer to her. There are no sharp objects near her, unless she plans on smacking me with a photo frame, so I think I'm okay being near her.

"What happened?" Reaching out, I brush the back of my fingers along her cheekbone. Her skin is soft under my hand and for a second, Scarlett's eyes close and she tilts her head into my hand.

She opens up so easily, like a flower blooming under the sun. When she lowers those walls, she built around herself, she's the softest angel.

Her eyes open and she glares at me. "Don't think I forgive you."

"I wouldn't dream of making that assumption."

"I still hope you choke on those damned cupcakes," she says.

"I'll get on it as soon as you tell me what's wrong."

Scarlett sighs and--to my regret--pulls away from me. Moving around me, she walks around the living room, inspecting every little thing closely. It's strange to picture her here, a place I avoided her being.

"I went to the Butter & Bloom today to make sure my sister's cake was going to be delivered on the wedding day, as planned." Scarlett turns to look at me, anger shimmering in her eyes once again. She crosses her arms. "Shane told me that my order had mysteriously disappeared from their system, even though I paid a deposit and received a confirmation."

"Is Shane still with us?"

"Of course. I wasn't going to harm him surrounded by witnesses, especially when the woman in the kitchen seemed to be pulling the strings."

That would be Jane. My ex. From *high school.* When I moved back, Marion told me to keep my distance because I was going to give a lot of people a lot of false hope because they'd assume I was somehow available. Especially because I decided to stay.

"I'll talk to her."

Scarlett looked at me flatly. "I don't want a cake from some woman who thinks she's in love with you. She's probably going to poison it. It'll be the most interesting thing that's probably happened in this town since you."

I walk closer to her, and she rounds the couch, walking further away. "Are you jealous, baby girl?'

Scarlett laughs humorlessly. "She can have you. I only need you until my sister is married."

I step in her way so she can't escape. She's pressed against the corner by the windows, the light streaming in from outside making her blue eyes appear clear as glass.

Leaning in, I brush her hair over her shoulder, letting my fingers graze along her pulse point. Her pulse jumps under my hand, pupils dilating as she stares up at me. She smells like sweet jasmine and warm sandalwood and it's the most intoxicating scent.

"You don't have to lie to me, hellion," I whisper. "I know you're angry, rightfully so, but there's no need for lies in our relationship."

If looks could kill, my family would be planning my funeral right now.

"We're *not* in a relationship, Connor."

"Not right now, at this moment." I lean in even closer, until our noses almost brush.

"Not ever," she protests. "What's done is done."

She arches up, closer to me, her eyes focused on my mouth. Fuck, I want to kiss her. My body craves her like sustenance. The heat radiating from her body, the scent of her perfume, the softness of her skin are an intoxicating mixture.

"Connor," she breathes.

I press my mouth against hers. Scarlett makes a sound, her hands coming up to my chest. Instead of pushing me away, though, she wraps her fists around my shirt and pulls me in closer. Mouth parting softly, she allows me access to taste her and now I'm the one who's moaning.

Scarlett is arching up, pressing her body against mine, one hand thrust in my hair. She tastes as sweet as I remember, like a rare delicacy. My mind is playing tricks on me and filtering out the last year and a half, almost as if it doesn't want to remember the time I spent without her.

"We can't," Scarlett murmurs on my lips. "I still don't forgive you."

But she's still kissing me. Still pushing her hand into the back pocket of my jeans and pulling me closer to her, rocking against my erection.

"And yet you're still fucking insatiable."

In response to that, she bites my lip, not enough to draw blood, but definitely enough to leave an impression.

Pushing me away, she walks to the other side of the room, her back to me as she takes a deep breath.

"Scarlett--"

"Don't play with me, Connor," she says, her voice hard. "This is hard enough as it is."

"I'm not fucking playing, Scarlett," I growl.

She turns, her hair flying like a purple curtain, lips bruised from my kiss. "Don't forget to eat the cupcakes." Her smile is fake and sugary. I guess we're still not talking about us, not even after that kiss. My skin suddenly feels too tight, and I can't wait another second, let alone days, to hold her again. I also know I'm pushing her too far too fast, and that way lies disaster.

"If I die, I won't be able to help with your sister's wedding," I say.

Scarlett laughs. "Oh, don't worry about that, if you die, I'm going to drag you back from hell. Now that that's settled, I have to go fight with your lover."

"If you mean Jane, she's not my lover."

The horrified look which crosses her face makes me laugh. "Jane and Shane? Small towns are so weird." Scarlett chews on her lip. "I think they're trying to ruin our stay because they think I hate you. We need to prove to them that everything is fine."

I'm standing by the arched entry of the living room and Scarlett pauses on her way out, tilting her head back to look at me. There's a turbulence of emotions in her eyes and I know I'm responsible for all of them. As if getting her back isn't going to be hard enough, the whole town is conspiring against me now.

"We should go to the Christmas Market, if you haven't

already. It's a good place to be seen and that should convince everyone that everything is fine."

"I don't know how I'm going to explain you to my family," she says.

"You mean I'll finally get to meet them?" I ask. Her arched eyebrow tells me she doesn't miss my sarcasm. "Look at that, all it took was a break-up and a botched wedding."

Grumbling something under her breath, Scarlett looks away, her cheeks coloring a faint pink. Even when we were together, I never worried that she didn't introduce me to her family. I certainly didn't want to introduce her to mine. Regardless of all that, I knew I was going to marry her, and nothing was ever going to keep me away, so whether or not I met her family was a moot point.

"I'll see you tonight at six outside the Inn," Scarlett says.

"I'll be there, baby girl."

"Stop calling me that!" With a look over her shoulder, she walks into the kitchen, presumably to get Harvey.

I'm wrong. The town isn't working against me. This stupid little boycott of theirs is going to work in my favor because now I don't have to worry about how I'm going to see Scarlett.

ELEVEN
SCARLETT

I know I've made a huge mistake inviting Connor to the Christmas market based on how my family reacts. As in, they're over the moon, thrilled, ecstatic, my mother probably thinks this is the best thing that's ever happened to me.

"What are you going to wear?" she asks, when I tell them. She's lounging on her bed while dad, Sienna, and Sadie play scrabble. We had plans to go to Calgary today again since I missed out the last time, but they're predicting a lot of snow tonight so we're leaving it for another day. It's a two-hour drive there and we should have started it this morning as opposed to the middle of the afternoon.

I carefully left out the part about Sienna's wedding cake order being cancelled, or the fact that we no longer have bouquets. And if that wasn't enough, we also no longer have the restaurant booking for the rehearsal dinner. This town is a cult and they all worship at the altar of Connor Hayes.

For a brief moment, I think I can't really blame them. That's clearly the kiss talking because I do blame them and him. This cult is ruining my sister's wedding and Connor is ruining my mind with his brain melting kisses.

Holy fuck, I forgot what it was like to kiss him. His mouth had been soft and firm, demanding access to mine in an all too familiar way. I hated to admit that it felt...right. My body had eased against his as if I'd been waiting for him.

I'm so confused. And my mother is not helping.

"You know he broke my heart, right?" I ask my mother.

Mom frowned, looking at my sisters and dad. I hadn't told them what happened, but I might as well. It's not like it's a big secret they can't know.

"We dated for six months and one day, I went to his apartment and the doorman handed me a letter from Mr. Hayes. Apparently, he'd packed up a bag and left in a hurry. There was no call, no message. Connor was just gone."

"That fucker," Sienna hisses.

Mom wraps an arm around me and pulls me against her. "Oh, baby. I'm so sorry."

Sienna and Sadie jump onto the bed and hug me and mom. "Daddy, come on," Sadie urges.

Dad gets onto the bed behind mom and wraps his arm around us. "I knew I didn't like that man."

Mom kisses my temple, and my body relaxes into the mattress, giving into the family embrace. While the hug goes a long way in calming the turmoil inside my chest, it also reminds me that Connor makes me feel the same way.

He's the only person other than my parents and sisters I have trusted enough to be completely at ease with. For the first two months of our relationship, it shocked me how much I wanted to give in, to not hold myself back from him.

"What was in the letter?" Sienna wonders.

"She's never read it," Sadie says. "It's still in her purse, sealed."

"What?!" The word is echoed by mom, dad, and Sienna. Their eyes swing to me, and I glare at Sadie. I told her that in confidence, but I guess she no longer feels like she has to keep it since I'm talking about Connor.

"Shouldn't we be focusing on Sienna? The one who's here to get married?" I ask.

"What's there to talk about? I locked Luke down in the ninth grade," Sienna says. She sits up and twists her long dark hair into a knot before crossing her legs under her and facing me.

"You, sister dear, are the real problem. What do you mean you haven't read Connor's letter? He could have explained why he left."

"Oh, come on," Dad scoffs. "He couldn't pick up a phone or send a message to explain why he left? He came to Alberta. He didn't go into witness protection."

I wave a hand toward dad. "Exactly. At least one person is on my side."

Sadie sits up, pushing her hair behind her ear. Mom remains next to me, brushing her fingers through my hair.

"Okay, can we establish that we're not Connor fans?" Sadie says. We all nod. "Excellent. That being said, isn't there a possibility of there being a totally valid explanation for why he left?" She holds up her hands. "I'm not saying he did the right thing or that he couldn't have called or messaged. I'm just saying, there has to be a reason why he left."

I chew on my bottom lip. "I guess his grandfather got sick." My voice is soft as I say it. "When Marion said Christmas was her husband's favorite holiday and he died two years ago, that kind of aligns to when Connor left. But again, that begs the question of why not just tell me."

"There's an easy way to find out," Mom says. "Just ask him."

"I'd rather not," I say. It'll be like opening a can of worms and I already know anything he says is not going to be enough.

"Don't be a chicken," Sadie says. "If you don't ask him, we will."

These people have never heard of boundaries. I'm worried if I ask him and he says he left because his grandfather was dying, my anger will ebb a little and I don't want that. I want to continue being angry at Connor for as long as possible because that will mean I'm not going to get my heart broken again.

"What are you going to wear?" Mom asks softly, again. "You need something with a little oomph, a little sexy and come hither."

She does an overexaggerated pout and twists her body, pushing in her shoulders to highlight her cleavage--while wearing a turtleneck.

My sisters and I watch her in horror.

"Okay, well, we won't be doing any of that," Sienna says. "But I agree with wearing something sexy and come hither."

"I don't want to hear that," Dad protests, cringing.

"I'm going to wear my cable knit turtleneck and the barrel jeans with boots," I say, off the top of my head. It's the least sexy outfit I can think of, and it will cover everything. Problem solved.

I FORGOT that I don't live in a democracy because I don't get to wear what I want. Instead, I'm shoved into tights and a chocolate velour short skirt paired with brown boots and an oversized sweater.

"We still have to be mindful of the weather," I reminded my sister when they held up a corset top.

Sadie blow dries my hair into big waves while Sienna does

my make-up, as if I'm incapable of doing both those things. It reminds me of my second date with Connor when we drank champagne as they got me ready for the date. Back when they didn't know his name and thought he was just a cute guy I met outside the arena.

That was a fun night on all counts. Connor took me to see a concert by a popular pop princess, who was trying out some new songs in a small venue. He held me close, and kept the people away, making sure my drinks were fresh and safe. He was always so mindful of who was around me, like he expected someone to attack me when people were more likely to focus on him.

"Can you guys please be normal?" I ask my family, when we're all dressed.

"We'll try our best, but we can't make any promises," Mom says.

She hooks her arm through mine and leads me down the hallway to the stairs. Voices drift up to us as we go down the stairs and we find Connor and Marion talking in the lobby. When Connor looks up, I have this surreal thought like my family is giving me away to him.

It makes me want to run back up the stairs.

The corner of his mouth turns up just a little, and I think he's having the same thought. Only he likes it. What is this bizarre idea he has that we're getting back together? I suppose telling him that we have to spend time together doesn't help me.

"Connor," I say in greeting.

"Hellion," he replies. I guess it's better than baby girl.

I turn, introducing him to my family. He's as charming and courteous as I expected him to be.

"My, you're tall," Mom says, tilting her head back to look at him. "Kissing must have been a real back bender."

"Mom!" I cry, cringing hard.

"I didn't mind," Connor said, amicably. "It was like a reward."

Everyone beams at me, except dad who's still skeptical, and I roll my eyes. I can do without the cheesiness.

"Shall we go? We don't want to miss all the fun."

I push everyone towards the front door, which leaves me right in front of Connor we exit. He's wearing jeans and a thick sweater under a black jacket paired with black boots. Damn, he looks delicious enough to eat. I'm never going to survive tonight or the next week.

As we're about to walk out, he leans down to whisper in my ear. His scent surrounds me, and I breathe him in, clean, crisp air and the hint of something smoky.

"You look beautiful, baby girl," he says, the rasp in his voice sending shivers down my back. "Did you do this for me?"

"Don't be ridiculous, Connor," I say, "I did it for me. And for the cute guy I'm going to find for a vacation fling."

Connor's laugh follows me out of the Inn and to the car.

TWELVE
SCARLETT

The Christmas market is exactly as I expect. It's charming and feels like something out of a fairytale. In the middle of town square, there's a twenty feet tall tree, with a crystal star sparkling at the top.

The market spreads out over several blocks, fairy lights strung over the top. The air is scented with nutmeg and cinnamon. And the crowd. There are so many people here and I feel overwhelmed. I'm not good with crowds.

"Ooh, hot chocolate," Sadie says, pointing towards a stall. "Let's go."

My family heads in that direction and I fall behind. Connor stays by my side, his hand resting on the small of my back. He's so tall, and he can be intimidating when he needs to be, so no one comes within five feet of us.

"What would you like, baby girl?" He asks. "Any preferences or do you want to be surprised?"

"I think I've had enough surprises on this trip," I say, looking up at him. "But I guess a hot chocolate surprise can't be that bad. Unless you poison it."

Connor smiles at me. "Baby girl, you're the only one in this relationship who wants to commit murder."

Before I can tell him not to call me baby girl and remind him that we're not in a relationship, he's stepping up to the stall and ordering me a hot chocolate. Mom comes up to me, wrapping her arm around my waist as we watch Connor order hot chocolates and chocolate pistachio croissants.

"He's so nice," Mom whispers. "Not that I support him. I think that needs to be made very clear. I am on your side."

"I know, mama."

I never said Connor isn't nice. His kindness and generosity are two of the things which attracted me to him. He always went out of his way to help people, and I saw that first hand.

Connor comes back to us with my sisters in tow, all of them carrying hot chocolates and baked goods. I take my drink out of Connor's hand, our fingers brushing against each other.

I take a tentative sip of my hot chocolate and realize it tastes like hazelnut and cinnamon. It's perfectly hot and it warms me from the inside. Connor watches me drink with satisfaction coloring his eyes. Ugh, I hate that he knows me so well.

"So, Connor," mom says. "Do you miss hockey? I mean, you were such a big star."

We continue walking, Dad and Mom holding hands, Sadie with her arm hooked through Sienna's. With everyone coupled off, it leaves me next to Connor. I shove my free hand into the pocket of my coat so that it doesn't brush against his. If no one else is going to maintain the distance between us, then I'm going to do it myself.

"I do," Connor says. "But there are people in New York I miss more."

I feel everyone glance at me, but I keep my eyes forward. I don't want to think about Connor missing me.

"Is it just you and Marion in the family?" Mom asks. I shoot her a look. She doesn't need to go through this third degree with Connor.

"You don't have to answer that," I say, looking up at him. Connor's eyes meet mine and, in their depths, I see his gratitude.

"I didn't mean to pry," Mom says. "Scarlett is right, you don't have to answer."

Pulling my hand out of my pocket, I brush my fingers against Connor's hand.

"I don't mind," he says. "My parents died when I was young, my grandfather died two years ago. He raised me and my brothers. Now it's just me, Marion, and my brothers left."

"How many brothers do you have?" Sienna asks.

Two. Wyatt, the middle brother, and Finn, the youngest. I already know the answer because he's mentioned them to me. I never met them, though I knew what they were like to some extent.

"Two brothers," Connor says. "I'm the oldest."

"Being the oldest child is not easy," Sienna agrees. "Unless and especially if you have a Scarlett as your sister."

"I'm delightful," I say. "You're grateful to have me and you know it."

"You're certainly a delight, angel," dad says. "But you also got into a lot of fights in school, and you never listened to your teachers."

"I was fighting bullies, and Miss Cartwright was having an affair with the principal, so I didn't feel the need to listen to her."

They laugh and I sip my hot chocolate. Connor and I are close enough that our hands keep brushing. I have this feeling like I'm playing with fire, but I can't stop. When he wraps his pinky finger around mine, I don't pull back.

"Oh, look at those pretty Christmas ornaments," Sadie points out.

Just as we start to move toward a stall, someone calls out Connor's name. We turn to see a middle-aged woman ambling towards us.

"Marion told me you'll be around," she says, beaming up at him. "Can you do me a favor? I need help getting something from the back and I don't know where Mike's disappeared to."

"No yeah, lead the way." He stops and turns to me. "I'll be right back."

I nod and watch him walk off with the woman. He's stopped two more times by people who recognize him and also somehow need his help.

"I just realized that you dated the popular jock," Sienna says. "You hated jocks."

We enter the store where the rest of our family disappears into. Sadie and mom are inspecting Christmas ornaments while dad stands by, listening to their conversation. Sienna and I stand back from them.

"I hate the stereotypical jock," I point out. "The kind who's too dumb to survive or who's smart but thinks he can do no wrong because he can throw a ball around or hit a piece of rubber with a stick."

Sienna looks at me with introspective hazel eyes. "You really liked him, didn't you?"

"I loved him," I admit. I'm sure they've already figured it out and since I'm spilling all my secrets today, I may as well tell her.

"I can't imagine how I'll react if Luke suddenly left without a word," she says, frowning.

I can't imagine it, either. Maybe because I can't imagine Luke leaving her. The way he looks at Sienna, I don't think it's even occurred to him that he might find someone else. It's Sienna or no one else.

"He'll be here soon," I say, pushing my shoulder against hers.

She grins at me, her whole face lighting up. "I can't wait. You and Sadie will definitely need some noise cancelling headphones."

"Gross!" I shove her away, laughing. She shoves me right back and I lose my balance on my delicate heels, reaching out my arm to grab something. Sienna reaches for me just as my hand is gripped in a warm, calloused one, and my back meets a solid wall of a body.

"Are you okay, baby girl?"

I look up at Connor and find him frowning at me in concern.

"I'm fine," I say. "She's been trying to get rid of me since we were kids."

Sienna laughs. "If only it was that easy."

Connor doesn't release me that easily. His arm is still wrapped around my waist, hand still in mine. My eyes drop to his mouth, and I can't help remembering the kiss from this afternoon.

It made me realize that I miss the feel of his body pressed against mine. It always made me feel safe and protected. I take Krav Maga classes, and I can defend myself if I need to, but it's nice knowing that I don't need to when he's with me.

That's the kind of thing I shouldn't be thinking if I hope to survive this wedding with my heart intact.

I step away from him and next to Sienna, grabbing her hand. She squeezes it once, letting me know she's on my side. No matter what my family says to me, or teases me about Connor, I know in the end, they will always be on my side.

"Everything go okay?" Sienna asks.

"Yeah, Cathy just needed help with a couple of boxes."

"You should buy some Christmas decorations," I tell him. "Since there are none in your house."

"When were you in his house?" Sienna asks.

Connor and I exchange looks and he raises an eyebrow in challenge. I take a bracing breath and look at my sister.

"Don't panic, but we kind of hit a snag with all our bookings."

Sienna blinks in confusion. "I'm sorry, what does that mean? What kind of snag? Which bookings?"

"It's my fault," Connor says. "Apparently the town has decided that Scarlett is the villain in our break-up and they've cancelled your bookings."

Sienna opens her mouth, closes it, opens it again. Turning to me, she places both hands on my arms and meets my eyes. "Is this true? Do these people hate us because of him?"

"I'm going to fix it, Si. No one is going to mess up this wedding," I say with all the conviction I can muster.

"I'm not a bridezilla and I can't care less about my wedding right now," Sienna says. "Luke and I can get married in town hall for all I care. I don't want to get married in a town where people villainized my sister over some man."

Feeling a surge of gratitude, I hug her, and she clutches me to her with strong, protective arms. Having sisters is like having built in friends. As much as we fought growing up, we're each other's best friend and would kill for the other, no questions asked.

"Why am I not invited to the sister hug?" Sadie is suddenly next to us, and we open our arms, pulling her in.

"You're going to have the wedding of your dreams," I promise Sienna. "That's why Connor is here." I look at him over her shoulder. "If he messed it up, then he's going to fix it. Even if he has to learn how to bake a cake and become a florist."

THIRTEEN
CONNOR

This woman doesn't know the depths I'll go for her. Because if she wants me to become a baker and a florist in the next seven days, I'll make it happen. Hell, I've already got a florist booked for her.

I've been playing hockey since I was a kid and the one thing hockey taught me is how much I like to win. And I'll do whatever it takes to win Scarlett back.

They pull apart from their sister hug and Sienna's demeanor towards me is a lot colder. I'm not upset at losing whatever ground I'd gained in the past hour. Even though they frustrate me to no end, I still love my brothers and if this town turns against them, they'll have to deal with me.

We exit the store and continue walking around the market. It's been the same since I was a kid. My parents used to bring us here every year for the tree lighting and my grandfather continued the tradition. I feel a lot of guilt over leaving him, and at the same time, I know that I needed to leave because back then, this town wasn't the place for me.

"Do you like living here, Connor?" Kate asks. I turn to Scarlett's mother and find her looking at me.

"When I'm here, I miss the anonymity of New York. When I was there, I missed the quiet mornings of Silverpine," I say.

"But do you like living here?" She asks again.

She has the same tenacity in her eyes that I see in Scarlett's. I remember Scarlett mentioned her mother used to be an investigative journalist. On the other hand, her father, Patrick, has remained quiet, just watching and listening and I can see where Scarlett gets that quality. Holding herself apart even when she's part of the crowd.

"I'm not sure. Being here comes with a lot of responsibility and reminds me that I left for a reason. But Cedar Creek has been in my family for generations and it's now my responsibility."

I feel Scarlett's eyes on me from where she is walking with her sisters. It's a lot of information I'd already shared with her, about never wanting to come back because I wanted to play hockey.

"You have brothers," Kate points out. "Can't one of them take care of Cedar Creek?"

"They can't even take care of themselves," I say, bitterness seeping into my voice.

"I'm sure it's not easy being the only responsible one," Kate says.

Responsibility isn't supposed to be easy. My grandfather used to say that to me every time I called. Marion still says that to me, but if I leave tomorrow, she wouldn't mind. She'd probably tell me I should have left a long time ago.

"Should we take photos with the Christmas tree?" Sadie asks. "Since our trip to the Rockefeller can't happen because someone had to get married at Christmas."

"I'm not coming to your wedding," Sienna quips back.

"I'm going to get married in the town hall," Sadie shoots back.

Scarlett laughs. "You're probably going to have a bigger wedding than Sienna's. *Everyone* you've ever met will be invited."

"I like meeting people!" Sadie protests.

We stop in town square, in front of the tree and I take a step back as the Monroe sisters have their photo session. It's interesting to see Scarlett with her family, something I never got to see. She's different with people, more closed off. But seeing her with them makes me realize she was never closed off with me. She allowed me to see parts of herself others don't get to see.

I got to see her fears and insecurities. I got to stay up with her at night because she had insomnia and couldn't sleep. There were nights we'd stay awake and play cards or board games. Nights where we'd watch endless movies, and she'd sit beside me crocheting. Nights where she'd wake me up with her hands and mouth and I'd push into her warm body and there were no words spoken, our bodies doing all the talking.

Christ, how I miss her. If she comes back to me, I'll never let her go. I'll insist on dying first so I never have to be without her.

"Connie!"

I wince at the sound of the ridiculous nickname, turning to look at Jane. Her blonde hair is pulled into a high ponytail, and her cheeks are flushed pink from the cold. We've been friendly with each other since I came back but I've always kept my distance because I'm not interested in rekindling any relationship. When I left at eighteen, everyone believed I was leaving Jane behind and would come back for one day.

"Jane." I nod at her, turning back to look at Scarlett. Her eyes are on us as Patrick takes Sienna and Sadie's photo and Kate helps a family with theirs.

"I didn't expect to see you here," Jane says. "You haven't been to the market since you came back, not even to see the tree lighting."

"I've been busy," I say.

"I'm sure it's not easy being back here without your grandfather. I'm so happy you're here." Jane smiles up at me warmly and my stomach clenches with unease, especially when she lifts a hand and squeezes my bicep in comfort.

"I came here for Scarlett," I say, my eyes swinging back to her.

Jane follows my gaze, and her smile drops when she sees Scarlett walking up to us.

"You came here for a woman who probably doesn't even care about you?" Jane inquires.

"No, I came here for the woman I love," I say.

Jane flinches, shock flickering across her face. I don't want to be rude and I'm not going to compare the two women. But Jane needs to understand that I'm never going to want her or anyone else the way I want Scarlett. This is just the Christmas market. I will go to the ends of the Earth if Scarlett asks me to.

"We're waiting for you to take pictures," Scarlett says, walking up to us. She slips her hand into the crook of my elbow as she steps up next to me. I look down at her hand on my arm and raise an eyebrow in question.

She's not jealous, but she doesn't give up the chance to stake her claim.

"I was just catching up with Jane," I say.

Scarlett looks at her, blue eyes hardening with anger. She smiles, but it doesn't reach her eyes. "We've never met, but you cancelled the order for my sister's wedding cake," she says.

"Technical errors happen," Jane says, her smile just as brittle.

"I can't imagine how much business you must lose with

technical errors," Scarlett says. "That happened at our shop once. We'd received an order for ten chocolate pies and lo and behold, the system deleted the order even though the confirmation had been sent. Luckily, the customer called the day before to follow up on when they should pick up the order and we were able to get it out on time. Customer service is very important when you're running a business."

If she'd cut Jane, it would have bled less. My girl can be savage when she needs to be.

"We're very busy during the holiday season and I don't believe in overworking my employees," Jane says, her tone sharp as cut glass.

Scarlett laughs lightly, her fingers digging into my arm. She's so beautiful I can't look away from her. I should step in and stop this fight, but Jane brought this on herself. There was no need to involve feelings with her business and I'd never been able to stop Scarlett.

"I agree. Which is why we try to make a lot of the orders ourselves at our shop. If it's our mistake, it shouldn't be our employee's responsibility to solve it. Everyone has different priorities and SOPs for running their business." Scarlett sighs. "Anyway, I'll stop by tomorrow."

"For what?" Jane blinks in confusion.

"To get my deposit back, of course. Since there's not going to be an order, there doesn't need to be a deposit. I'm sure you wouldn't want your business reported for fraudulent activity."

Tugging on my arm, Scarlett pulls me away.

"We'll see you tomorrow," I tell Jane.

She watches us in shock as Scarlett tugs me away to stand in front of the tree with her, Sadie taking our photo.

"I wasn't sure I'd be invited to take photos," I say.

Feeling her gaze on me, I turn to look down at Scarlett. The bright lights of the Christmas tree are reflected in her clear eyes as she watches me. I'm surprised to see the hint of possessiveness in them, the way her hand tightens on my arm, and she pulls me closer.

"Only I get to call you Connie," she says.

The smile that steals across my face would be visible from the moon. She doesn't want me, but she can't stop her jealousy. That has to be a good thing, right? If another man called her cute nicknames, I don't know what I'd do. Probably be arrested for assault.

"Don't worry, baby girl. I didn't rig my washroom with the best surround sound speakers so I can listen to her erotic audios as I rub one out in the shower every day."

Scarlett gasps loudly, choking on air. "Connor! You didn't!" She's horrified.

I laugh, even though it's not a laughing matter. "I don't think you realize how obsessed I am with you, Scarlett."

A blush steals across her pale cheeks and Scarlett ducks her head. If we weren't surrounded by people and her family, I'd tilt her head back and kiss her again.

"Alright, photo session is over," Sadie announces. "Where are we going?"

"Let's find something to eat, I'm starving," Sienna says.

"Me, too."

Scarlett releases my arm and goes to her sisters. Stopping halfway, she throws a look over her shoulder. "Coming?"

"We'd both be, if you weren't so stubborn," I say quietly.

Amused blue eyes turn up to me. "You've grown awfully bold."

"Patience is a young man's game. I'm practically geriatric."

"You're thirty-eight," she points out.

"Which means I've only got a handful of years left before my mid-life crisis."

Her family leads the way as we trail behind. There are a lot of tourists in the Christmas market, but I still feel the town's eyes following us as we walk past. I can picture Jane texting her mother about Scarlett's audacity and from there the news will spread down the grapevine. The librarians are always the first to know everything because they are the source of information.

"What does a mid-life crisis look like for you?" Scarlett asks.

"I can tell you what people imagine my mid-life crisis will be like, and by people, I mean my brothers," I say.

"I'd love to hear it."

"I'm going to buy a Corvette and I'm going to take full advantage of being Connor Hayes. As in, I'm going to invite women for a tour of Cedar Creek Ranch, spend the night with them, rinse and repeat."

Scarlett makes a face. "I can't picture it. The Corvette or the women. You'd probably keep bees."

I look at her from the corner of my eyes and Scarlett laughs.

"Oh my gosh! You keep bees, that's so adorable."

"If you need a full hazmat suit to deal with them, it's not adorable."

Scarlett tries to quell her laughter, shaking her head. "Oh, no, it's very manly."

"I know it's not a gendered activity and I don't need to feel manly. It's also not adorable."

We walk in silence for a few minutes. Sadie calls back that we're going to Salvatore's for dinner. Salvatore's would probably have a line out the front door because it gets busy quickly and I tell them to use the back door. I know the owner and the Hayes family are always welcome, no matter how busy the restaurant gets.

"You really do have connections with everyone," Scarlett says.

"My family founded Silverpine," I explain. "Whenever

anyone was struggling with anything, my grandfather was the first one to help them, sometimes to his own detriment. They see me as a part of them, something I can't ever get rid of. Feels like a horror movie sometimes."

"I'm really sorry about your grandfather," Scarlett says quietly.

I look at her. "Someday, when you're ready, I'll tell you why I left."

Scarlett's expression betrays nothing of what she's feeling. All she says is, "Maybe someday."

It's not a promise or a commitment, but it's still more than we've had so far. Her face makes it clear that I can't ask for more right now.

FOURTEEN
CONNOR

I wake up earlier than usual and take Midnight for a ride. I try to exercise each horse every day unless it's too cold, but I didn't have a good night's sleep and I'm feeling too jittery. I trust Midnight and he trusts me. I can ride him blindfolded.

The wind chases us, but Midnight is faster. I have to be careful though because it's still dark out and there's always a risk of hitting ice. I don't stay out too long, and I don't push Midnight too hard.

Once he is back in the stable and I've removed the saddle and given him a rub down, I make my way back to the house. After a quick shower, I fill two thermoses, one with hot chocolate and the other with coffee and take them out to the car.

This isn't part of my duty. Scarlett hasn't asked me to do this, and no one is going to see us so early in the morning. But she's stubborn and she still wants to run, even though it's dark, cold, and icy. I've been following her on her runs and I'm sure she's caught me more than once.

I pull up to the Honeysuckle just as Scarlett and her father step out. Scarlett is dressed in all black, a knit cap over her head. She laughs at something her father says, and when her eyes meet mine, she freezes.

"Connor? What are you doing here? Are you here to see Marion?"

"I'm here for you. I figured if you're going to go running in the morning, you need to have someone with you."

Her mouth opens and closes. "You're going running with me?"

"If you want me to."

"She really prefers to run alone," Patrick says.

"I'm just trying to make sure she's safe," I say.

"That's what I'm there for," her father replies.

I guess I really am Public Enemy number one. I don't blame any of them for being angry or upset. It must be the way that I've been raised, in a town that's always praised my family, that I'm having a hard time wrapping my mind around their stubbornness to even listen.

"Maybe he can drive along with you," Scarlett suggests to her father. There's a malicious gleam in her eyes that tells me she's not doing this as a favor for me. She expects her father to give me a hard time and that's the only reason she's asking for this.

He agrees, and I transfer the thermoses from my truck to his car. We watch in silence as Scarlett warms up for her run. I get in the car with her father when she starts a slow jog down the street.

"Just so you know, your approval rating is in the mid-twenties," Patrick says.

I turn to him. "I was expecting it to be lower than that, so I'm grateful. Who voted for me?"

He looks at me from the corner of his eyes. They're the same icy blue as Scarlett's and just like his daughter, I see his emotions hidden behind them. "Kate is on the fence. But the rest of us are quite sure you're bad news. Because of you, one of my daughters is heartbroken and the other one's wedding is being ruined."

If I was a father, and in his position, I would have knocked myself out by now. The fact that he's being courteous enough to let me in his car says a lot about his character.

"Mr. Monroe, I can assure you I have no intention of ruining your daughter's wedding. And as for Scarlett's broken heart, it's not something that I did intentionally, and it's something that I'll regret my whole life. I had a choice to make, and I thought I made the right one. Leaving Scarlett wasn't easy for me, but allowing her to deal with the mess that was going to be my life here wasn't going to be fair to her."

My grandfather was a good man, but he was also a demanding one. I didn't leave this town just for hockey. I left because I didn't want to be here. I didn't want to be under his thumb. I didn't want to spend my whole life chasing after my brothers because he spoiled them. And that's exactly where I am now, all because I owed the man who raised us. I came back out of duty and guilt, not out of love.

"You could have contacted her and told her that," Patrick says. "Or better yet, let her make the decision herself."

We roll to a stop as Scarlett waits for the pedestrian light to turn green. She glances back at us briefly before focusing her eyes ahead. I've always admired her dedication to running every day. Being an athlete isn't easy.

"You and I both know that Scarlett is stubborn and loyal to a fault. She would have thought she could handle it, but she was twenty-five. She shouldn't have had to handle anything. I wouldn't have been able to give her the time and attention a relationship needs, and it would have turned bitter regardless. The way I saw it, every option led us here."

Patrick sighs deeply, and eyes the thermoses. "You got coffee in one of these?"

I pour him a cup and we sit in silence for the rest of the ride, trailing behind Scarlett as she completes her run. I think the ice between her father and me thaws a little and it might help my approval rating, but who could tell.

I TOLD Scarlett to meet me at the Rusty Nail after breakfast. I'm not going to bake her sister's wedding cake, but I know someone who can.

"You know I don't do that anymore," Cam says, when I ask him to bake the cake.

"I know, which is why it'll be a huge personal favor to me if you did," I say, looking at him over the bar. He's cleaning glasses with a dish towel and setting them on the shelf behind him, getting ready for the day. The bar will have stragglers coming in the afternoon and as soon as five o'clock hits, it's going to be standing room only. More than once, Cam's been shut down by the fire department for being over capacity.

Its rustic charm drew in all the tourists, especially those who liked to get drunk and ride the mechanical bull in the back. A neon sign behind the bar read 'Sinners Welcome', the wood countertop was scratched and had seen better days, and it was often too dark in here.

It was exactly the kind of place one would expect shady deals to happen in. It was also the only business in Silverpine which didn't decorate for Christmas, a fact which earned Cam a fine each year. Because Silverpine's business association and the town's planning committee took their planning seriously. Since Christmas brought in a lot of tourists, they were determined to play up the season as much as possible.

Every year, decorations go up on November 12th like clockwork.

"Helping you get the girl isn't my idea of a favor," Cam says.

"I thought we're friends."

Cam sighs, running a hand over his red beard. "Let me think about it."

I don't have a lot of time for him to think about it because Scarlett is on her way. I don't want to give her half-answers and empty promises. That's a fact which has never changed about our relationship. If she wants something, she's going to get it.

A hand lands on my shoulder, and I look over to see Jared, the owner of Milnes Hardware, Jane's ex-husband, and my nemesis. Jared and I used to be friends, played in all the junior leagues together, went to university together in Toronto, right up until I was drafted to the NHL, and he wasn't. He came back to Silverpine instead of staying in Toronto, took over his family's hardware store, and married Jane. I think a part of him blames me for something and I can't understand why.

"Heard you're having lady trouble," Jared says. His dark eyes look almost gleeful.

I look at Cam and he rolls his eyes.

"No trouble," I say. "A little bit early for you to be in here, isn't it?"

"Saw your car in the parking lot and thought I'd come say hello to an old friend. Your friend really upset Jane last night."

"Is that why you're here? To defend your ex-wife?" I ask.

These are the kinds of things I was able to avoid in New York and Toronto. Because even though I was Connor Hayes, people didn't feel the need to be involved in every aspect of my life, and I was able to set stricter boundaries.

"She's the mother of my child, Connor. If someone upsets her, I have to react," Jared says.

All right, I can't blame him. If someone upsets Scarlett, I'm going to react the same way.

"She started this, Jared, by pretending she lost the order. I can't control the way Scarlett reacts." Behind him, I see Scarlett struggling to open the door with a huge binder in her arms. That's not what gives me pause. She's wearing my hat. I left it in her father's car this morning and now she's wearing it, not realizing what it means.

"Move," I say to Jared. "I have nothing else to say to you and if Jane has a problem, she can take it up with me herself."

Jared follows my gaze to Scarlett. "That her? Maybe I can talk to her myself."

"You take one step near her and you're going to regret it for the rest of your life," I growl. "*Move,* Jared."

Grinding his jaw, Jared vacates the stool next to me just in time as Scarlett reaches us and sets down the binder on the counter with a loud thunk. Cam watches us with amused eyes.

"Nice hat," he says, giving me a meaningful look.

"Thank you," Scarlett chirps. "I thought it'd look cute with my outfit."

"I'll be right back," he says, giving me another meaningful look.

"What's that all about?" Scarlett asks me. She removes her coat to reveal a green sweater she's paired with a black pleated skirt, black tights, and tall boots. I want to fuck her when she's wearing nothing but those boots and my hat.

"Baby girl, you walking around wearing my hat sends a certain message," I say.

"What message?" Scarlett blinks at me, wide-eyed. I turn in my stool, Scarlett's legs trapped between both of mine.

"It says you're mine to look at," I say. "Mine to touch, and please. My woman. It means when you wear that hat, you're making yourself mine. I don't have a habit of letting go of things that belong to me. I already made that mistake and I'm not going to make it again."

Scarlett swallows roughly, resting her hand on my thigh as she leans closer towards me. I breathe in her scent, reveling in the heat of her palm seeping through my jeans.

"I'm not yours, Connor," she whispers

"Not yet, baby girl."

I'm more certain than ever that before she leaves, she will be mine. I don't know what the future will look like, whether we'll both be in Silverpine or in New York. I do know that it doesn't matter where we are. We will be together. We can figure out the rest later.

She hums thoughtfully. "In other news, I went by Butter & Bloom on my way here and got my deposit back."

Suddenly, it makes sense why she's wearing my hat, and it makes me laugh. She's a menace, knowing exactly what it would mean if she wore my hat.

"Did you wear my hat on purpose, hellion?"

"How quickly I go from baby girl to hellion." Scarlett pouts.

"If you act like a hellion, you'll get called one."

Looking at me through the corner of her eyes, she says, "Are you upset?"

Reaching under, I grab the legs of her stool and pull her chair forward. Scarlett gasps, her hand tightening on my thigh and the other coming to rest on my chest. Scarlett tilts her head back to look at me, mouth parted in surprise.

"I can never be upset with you, Scarlett." I hold her gaze, letting her see the truth in my eyes. Slowly, I lean in and suck on her bottom lip. She moans softly, her hand fisting in my shirt and pulling me closer.

As angry as she still is with me, I'm also certain that she still wants me. I pull away from her, not wanting to push her too far.

"What's this?" I ask, nodding at the binder.

Scarlett's lashes flutter as she blinks rapidly and shakes her head lightly, as if trying to clear the brain fog. "This is the wedding book." She opens it and reveals the contents. "It's got everything. From potential venues, to flowers, to cakes, centerpieces, decor ideas, whether you want a big wedding or a small wedding, a built in guest list for the Monroe family."

I'm fascinated by the thoroughness and the multiple tabs. I'm even more fascinated by the fact that it's divided into three sections, one for each sister. Scarlett has a tab.

"This is your wedding book," I say.

Scarlett runs a finger along the edge of the tab which has her name on it. "It's not mine, specifically. It's for all three of us and mom built it around our personalities."

I reach for the book, lifting the page before her tab and Scarlett smacks my hand lightly.

"You can't see that," she admonishes.

"Why not? Considering I'll be the groom, I have every right to know what my wedding will look like."

Scarlett's jaw drops open in shock. Fuck, how I love teasing her.

"You're not going to be my groom, Connor," she says.

"Give me one good reason why not," I reply.

Scarlett releases a deep breath. "Because this isn't a movie and I'm not going to leave everything to move to a small town because you have a very niche business that can't be done anywhere else."

"Technically, I can't move the ranch to New York. We can buy a ranch in New York and leave Oliver to run things here. I'll have to come back a few times a year to make sure everything is running fine but other than that, it shouldn't be a problem."

As soon as the words leave my mouth, I regret them. Not because I don't mean them because I mean every word. I know

I left her to come here, but the past year and a half has made me realize I will leave Silverpine for Scarlett. Choosing her might make me selfish but I can't live without her. Maybe, just maybe, she can't live without me either.

"You left me to come back and now you're going to leave for me?" Scarlett questions. She doesn't look upset, which is saying a lot.

"Leaving here to be with you will be the easiest decision I'll ever make," I say with all sincerity. "Leaving you was the hardest decision and one I had no choice but to make."

Scarlett looks down at the wedding book, fingering the edge of the binder. This isn't a conversation I want to have here, where anyone can walk in. I feel Jared's gaze burning into my back.

"Cam is going to make your sister's cake," I say. Changing the topic is the best option.

"I haven't agreed, yet," Cam says from the other end of the bar.

Scarlet leans forward to look at him. "What can we do to convince you? I'll pay you the same rate that I was going to pay Jane."

"I'm not exactly worried about the money. Connor will pay me whatever I ask," Cam says, running a hand over his beard. "I'm not a baker anymore. I run a bar. I don't think I'm qualified for the job."

"As long as the cake is edible, we won't complain," Scarlett says. "But if you feel like it's too much, we won't pressure you."

Cam looks thoughtful, his grey eyes locked on Scarlett. He's my friend and I know he wouldn't try anything with Scarlett, but a part of me still wants to shield her.

"Come back here tonight and I'll prepare something for you," he finally says.

I straighten in my chair immediately. "Why tonight?"

The place is going to be loud and crowded, exactly the kind of place Scarlett hates. Exactly the kind of place I hate and don't want to be in. But if she's here then I'll have to be here because there's no way I'm going to leave her in a bar surrounded by drunk men hitting on her.

"Because I need time to bake something for her to try," Cam says, reasonably.

"Tonight is perfect. All the cousins are coming into town this afternoon and we need a place to celebrate the bride," Scarlett says excitedly.

I glare at Cam, and he winks at me. The asshole knows exactly what he's doing. Scarlett opens the wedding book again, drawing my attention to her.

"Next on the list is a place to have the rehearsal dinner," she says. "I don't know what the booking situation is like, but I was hoping we could do it at the lodge." She looks at me in question.

"It's yours, you don't even need to ask."

I'll tell Harvey to move around reservations as needed. Scarlett is a priority and her reservation comes first.

Since Cam has reluctantly agreed to make the cake, I tell Scarlett about the florist in Calgary. "We'll have to drive down there to meet with them. We can go tomorrow, if that works for you."

She chews on her bottom lip. "Are you sure they'll be available? The wedding is next week."

"Don't worry about it. I promised that I'm going to make sure your sister's wedding happens without a hitch and I intend on keeping that promise. Whatever you want is yours."

A blush blooms across her cheeks and Scarlett looks down, hiding it from me. She gets off her stool and picks up the wedding binder again.

"Well, since that's settled, I should get back to my family."

Walking to the end of the bar, she leans across the counter towards Cam. "Thank you so much for helping us. I can't wait to try what you come up with tonight. Can I give you my number, in case anything comes up you can give me a call?"

"For sure," Cam says, passing her a napkin to write her number on. Scarlett quickly scribbles her phone number and passes it back to him.

I watch the whole exchange, seething with jealousy. I'm the one who brought her here, so I have no one to blame other than myself. The way I see it, this is a win some lose some situation. If Jane hadn't canceled Scarlett's order, then Scarlett would never have come to me, and I never would have come to Cam.

I have no choice other than to accept the situation.

Scarlett turns to walk away, and stops, turning to face me. "Did you want the hat back?"

I'm acutely aware of Cam and Jared listening to this conversation. But I don't care because they might as well know, and they can tell the whole town as well.

"Nah, baby girl. The hat is yours now." I don't want there to be any questions about who she belongs to. I'm going to possess Scarlett, body, mind and soul.

FIFTEEN
SCARLETT

During the day, the Rusty Nail feels like it's a bar in the middle of nowhere. The kind of sketchy place you will stumble upon driving down the lone highway.

At night? It's the most exciting place in Silverpine. I'm sure there are more people here than the fire code allows, and we're packed in like sardines. It's hot and sweaty, and I'm suddenly so grateful that my sister's forced me into this corset top. I'm wearing my tightest pair of jeans paired with my boots. And of course, Connor's hat which he said belongs to me now.

I've recorded enough erotic audios and romance audiobooks to know exactly what it means for me to be wearing his hat. There was a reason I walked into Butter & Bloom wearing his hat. And yeah, part of it was jealousy. Hearing Jane call Connor by the nickname I gave him made me see red. I know he hates that stupid nickname just as much as I hate baby girl. But those are nicknames we gave to each other.

As far as I'm concerned, only I get to call him Connie, even if he hates it.

Our four cousins arrived for the wedding already, along

with our aunts and uncles and grandma. The parents and grandma are staying back at the Inn to watch Christmas movies while the cousins are at the Rusty Nail.

I push my way to the bar and see the cute bartender from earlier. "Cam!" I wave to him. He looks at me and finishes serving the customer before walking over to me.

"I see you're still wearing the hat," is the first thing he says.

I shrug lightly. "I think it looks cute."

"Connor isn't here yet, but I'm sure he's not far behind."

I roll my eyes. "I don't need Connor to babysit me. Now, what have you prepared for my sister?"

"Why don't you grab a table, and I'll bring it over to you?"

"We already grabbed a table. We're over there by the windows."

I point in the general direction of where our table is and Cam nods.

I make my way back to the table and sit down in my empty chair.

"I can't believe you're getting married. Meanwhile, I can't even get a second date with a decent guy," Mia is saying. At nineteen she's the youngest of the bunch so she doesn't really need to worry about not finding the love of her life yet. She's recently cut her hair into a cute bob, which looks adorable on her elfin features.

"You can't really compare yourself to Sienna, though," our other cousin, Julia, says. "She met the love of her life at fourteen because they were forced to work on a project together."

"How come none of my teachers forced me to work with a cute guy?" Mia says with the pout.

"Maybe the reason you can't find someone is because there's no one out there who can put up with you," Logan says, pushing a hand through his dark hair. At thirty-two, Logan is the oldest cousin. Next to him is his brother Caleb, who's thirty, like Sienna. Then it's me, then Julia, who's twenty-five, then Sadie, and finally Mia.

In a sea of dark-haired cousins, I stand out with my lavender hair. My aunt Helen told Mom that I should color my hair back to brown for the wedding because I wouldn't want to draw attention away from Sienna and look strange in the photos as the maid of honor.

But that's not something my sister has ever worried about. In fact, when I told her I was considering changing my color back to brown, she flat out told me that if I was doing it for the wedding, then I was going to be uninvited.

Cam brings over a small cake and seven spoons. The cake is absolutely gorgeous and so cute, pale butter yellow frosting covering the outside with white flowers.

He sets the cake and the spoons on the table. "Let me know what you think."

I push the cake towards Sienna since she's the bride, and her opinion is the only one that matters.

Slowly, my sister cuts off a piece and puts it in her mouth. Her eyes close as she lets out a little moan of delight.

"This might be the best cake that I've ever eaten," she says.

I turn to Cam and see that his cheeks are red over his beard. "You're hired. I'm going to send you the cake that we want. Let me know if you're able to make it. If not, we'll come up with something new."

I look to Sienna to confirm, and she nods.

"Connor came through on that," she says once Cam leaves.

"I'm pretty sure he has ulterior motives, but I don't care as long as he sticks to the plan."

His words from this afternoon echo in my mind.

Considering I'll be the groom, I have every right to know what my wedding will look like.

He said it's so easily, like it's already a done deal. Like I'm going to marry him. He hasn't even proposed, he hasn't even apologized. We have hashed nothing out. We haven't even talked about why he left. But suddenly he's talking about us getting married.

Thinking about it is just making me angry.

"Can we not talk about Connor?" I ask Sienna. "Let's just focus on you and make this a fun night."

Understanding colors her eyes and she nods. "Let me know if working with him is too much and I'll do all the work."

"It's not too much, I'm fine. Besides, it's my duty as the maid of honor."

The conversation turns to the last time the cousins were all together. It was during the summer when the family planned a trip to London, England. Caleb reminds us all that we forgot Mia on the bus and Mia teases him by reminding us all that Caleb had fallen in love with the receptionist at the hotel.

The bar fills up even more, and we decide that since we will be leaving in a few days, this is the perfect time for us to flirt and find a vacation fling. Not me, though. Because try as I might, I can't bring myself to flirt with any man who's here.

Sienna and I lean against the bar and watch as our cousins and Sadie flirt with people.

"Twenty bucks says Caleb is going to strike out," Sienna says, watching Caleb flirt with a blonde. He appears to be coming on a little too strong.

"I'm not going to make a losing bet," I say.

"What about Sadie?" We look at our sister and see her flirting with a tall, red-haired man. He's cute, definitely vacation fling worthy. From what we can see, he's not being gross and he's keeping a respectable distance between them. Sadie has her hand resting on top of her glass, protecting her drink.

Mia is leaning against a wall as a dark-haired boy leans in towards her. But she's smiling and looking happy, and the boy looks to be about her age, so we leave her be. I'm looking around the bar for Julia when my eyes swing over a man in the corner watching me.

At first, I think it's a creep, but I immediately realize it's not. When I look back, I see that it's Connor. He's sitting in a corner, which allows him a view of the entire bar. He's leaning back in his chair, his legs spread out in front of him, fingers covering his mouth as he watches me across the dark bar.

There's a possessive gleam in his eyes that I can feel even from across the room.

"I know we don't like the man but damn there's something about him, something about the way that he looks at you," Sienna says quietly next to me. She also noticed Connor.

I know exactly what she means. Connor looks at me like I already belong to him, no matter where I am or who I'm with. I'll never be able to shake him off. I'm his and nothing is going to change that.

And that just pisses me off. Because what do you mean that I'm yours if you're going to leave me without a second glance?

I drink the shot of tequila that's sitting in front of me.

"You know what, I'm single," I say. "I'm going to flirt with some guys."

Cam is standing next to us and happens to hear me. He laughs lightly and looks at Sienna. "Is she always like this?"

"You have no idea," my sister says.

"Rude," I say. If anything, they should be questioning Connor.

"Who do you think I should flirt with?" I ask Cam, making him just as complacent in my plan. He looks around the bar and finally his eyes land on a guy who's standing by one of the pool tables. He seems to be here with a group of friends.

"I've seen him looking at you."

"Thank you, Cam. You are a very good friend."

Cam looks at me with amusement. "Tell that to Connor when he tries to kill me."

I give Sienna a kiss on the cheek and walk across the bar to the man Cam pointed out. The whole time, I feel Connor's gaze following me. Is flirting a moot point when I'm still wearing Connor's hat? Maybe. But that's not going to stop me from doing it.

"Hi!" I say cheerfully when I walk up to the man.

He's in the middle of taking a sip of his beer and chokes. He flushes red as his friends laugh.

"I'm sorry, I didn't mean to startle you," I say.

"He's just not used to beautiful women walking up to him," one of his friends says. His eyes linger on the swell on my breasts over my top.

I look the man up and down. He's cute, messy dark hair, and soulful brown eyes. He's about six feet so not so tall that I'm going to get a crick in my neck looking up at him. "I find that hard to believe," I say with a quick flick of my eyes at his friend.

"I'm Scarlett," I say, in the voice I usually reserve for my erotic audios. It's deeper and raspier than my normal voice.

His face seems to get redder. "I'm Ryan."

"Nice to meet you, Ryan. Do you live here or are you just traveling?"

"One of my friends has family here. We're just visiting on our way to Whistler."

"Oh, cool. I've always wanted to go to Whistler. But I'm so scared of those slopes. Are you a skier?" I tilt my head, letting the edges of my hair brush against the top of my breasts.

"I'm not an expert, but I can ski."

"Maybe you can teach me sometime?" I look at him coyly.

This is just me flexing my flirting muscle and pissing off Connor. Otherwise, this man is doing nothing for me. He's cute, without a doubt. But the last man I dated is still looking at me like I belong to him. I gave him my heart and I never got over it.

When Connor looks at me, it's with the kind of possessiveness they write about in books. Even right now, I'm wondering how long it will take before he loses his patience.

Do I want him to lose his patience and come over here to stake his claim? Maybe. The idea makes my heart race faster. But Connor is too sensible to do something like that. I don't know why I'm trying to push him. Maybe because I need reassurance. If he wants me, how far is he willing to go to get me?

Julia suddenly appears next to me. "Did you know they have a mechanical bull here?" She's sweaty and exhilarated. "I've always wanted to ride one."

I look to my new friend. "What do you say? Should we go see some bull riding?"

"Only if you're planning on doing it?" Ryan asks.

I laugh teasingly. "Bold. Is the shy thing just an act, then?"

"Uh, not really," he says, blushing. "I don't really know why I said that."

"Well, now you've already said it," Julia says, with a wicked gleam in her eyes. "So, we may as well do it."

She grabs my hand and pulls me towards the back. Belatedly, I reach back and take Ryan's hand. If I'm doing this, I might as well commit.

The crowd is denser in the back and louder. When we push to the front, we see a girl riding the mechanical bull. It looks sexy and it looks dangerous. My sisters and Mia are also gathered on the other side, and I wave at them. Sienna shakes her head at me.

"I'm going next," Julia says excitedly.

We all cheer her on when she gets up on the bull. It starts slow and then picks up speed. There are a lot of men watching and cheering and for a second, I feel nervous for having committed to this.

"You're not seriously getting on that, are you?" Ryan asks.

Before I can reply, a voice from behind me says, "No, she isn't."

Even in the hot, sweaty bar, surrounded by all these people, I shiver at the sound of his voice. I look over my shoulder at Connor and find him glaring at me.

"Funny, I didn't realize you were the boss of me."

A muscle in his jaw ticks. "You've proven your point well enough. Don't push it too far."

"I haven't proven anything," I say, the challenge in my voice obvious.

Connor pinches the bridge of his nose between two fingers. "If you want to ride the damn bull, I can bring you back here after the bar closes."

The crowd cheers loudly for Julia and I arch onto my toes to whisper in Connor's ear. "I thought you were going to say I should just ride you."

His throat bobs with a swallow as his heated gaze meets mine. "Baby girl, you know I won't deny you anything."

"Excellent, then I'm going to ride the bull." I've forgotten all about Ryan.

Anger flickers in Connor's eyes. "If you get on that thing, I won't be held responsible for my actions."

Heat pools in my belly at the threat in his voice. I don't know what's happening to me. These are exactly the kind of public displays I hate, and which make me wonder if people get a thrill out of taking their personal lives to the streets. For me, it's not really the thrill of other people watching me. It's all about Connor watching me.

Julia gets off the bull and I walk forward, high fiving her.

Getting on the bull is so easy and the guy who's running it

turns it on once I'm situated. It bucks to life under me, and I hold on tight, letting my hips rock with the bull rather than being stiff and falling off. The crowd whoops and cheers but I look directly at Connor. His face is hardened in anger, but I can see the amusement in his eyes.

Suddenly, he's walking across the pit towards me, motioning for the bull to be turned off. Before I can protest, he throws me over his shoulder.

"Connor!" I cry out, clutching one hand to my hat so it doesn't fall off. Shouts ring out from the crowd, and I look up just long enough to see my sisters and cousins giving me a thumbs up. It's a good thing Caleb and Logan didn't see this display because there would have been a fight.

Connor carries me down a short hallway and into a room, the door closing behind us. He lowers me to my feet, tossing my hat aside and pushing me against the door as his mouth descends on mine in a hard, bruising kiss. I open my mouth, allowing him access as I grip his flannel shirt and pull him against me. Our mouths move with fervor against each other as we try to close all distance between us.

"You drive me fucking crazy," Connor says against my lips.

"You call me hellion for a reason," I remind him.

He growls, kissing me again. I slip my hands under his shirt, raking my nails over his taut stomach. Even though he's not a professional athlete anymore, he's still maintained the same physique.

Connor trails kisses down my neck, his teeth raking along my pulse point.

"You just had to wear this top," he growls against the top of my breasts, his breath fanning over my heated skin.

"You don't like it?" I tease. "I think it makes my boobs look amazing."

Connor sucks on the globe of my breast and I cry out,

rocking into him. The scratch of his beard against my soft skin heightens the sensations running through my body. My pulse pounds between my legs, matching the rhythm of my heart. I can feel his hard length pressing against my leg and I lower my hand, cupping him through his jeans.

"You're coming home with me," he says, voice roughened with lust.

"What? I don't get a say?" I ask, as he lowers his head and leaves another bruising kiss on my chest. He's marking me as his.

"You're trying to make me come in my jeans, gripping my cock like it belongs to you," he says wryly. "Do you have something else to add to that?" He watches me with eyes heavy-lidded with lust.

I want this. I want him. Pressing against me, into me, making me feel like I belong to him and only him. I don't know what's going to happen tomorrow or if everything is going to work out between us. I just know that for tonight, I want him.

"I'll have to tell my sisters and my cousins," I say.

"We'll do it now," he says, pulling away from me. I wait for doubt or fear to rise, but it doesn't. I'm not even second guessing my decision to leave with him.

I lean against the door, catching my breath and I watch him reach up and start to unbutton his shirt.

"I thought we're going to your house?" I frown at him.

"We are, hellion. I'm giving you my shirt to cover up, unless you want to walk out there like that." He looks at my chest and I follow his gaze to see the bruises blooming along the globes of my breasts.

"Oh my god, Connor! This is ridiculous."

Gently, he threads my arms through his shirt. It hangs on me like I'm a child. Connor slowly buttons it up, all the way, and then rolls the sleeves so my hands are free. He stands back with a self-satisfied look in his eyes.

I cross my arms, arching an eyebrow. "Are you happy now?"

"I warned you I won't be responsible for my actions," he said. "You didn't want to listen and still got on that thing."

I shift forward, sliding my hands over his t-shirt covered torso. Arching up, I place sucking kisses all over his neck.

"I bet you liked it, though," I murmur. "Seeing me up there, riding that bull. It brought back a lot of memories, didn't it?"

Growling, Connor lowers his mouth to mine. With one hand thrust into my hair, Connor tilts my head, giving him better access to my mouth. I part my lips, letting our tongues tangle and taste. He tastes like whiskey and bad decisions.

"We need to leave. Now, Scarlett." When he uses my name like that, I know he means business. Considering we're about to have sex in Cam's office, this is serious business.

"Can you get my sisters please? I don't want to go out there," I say. The insanity which made me bold enough to ride that bull has left and I'm suddenly acutely aware that the people out there probably think we fucked it out in here.

Connor frowns. "I don't want to leave you in here."

"There's no one here to harm me."

He still looks unsure, and it occurs to me that he probably thinks if he leaves me alone, the fog of lust will lift, and I'll change my mind about leaving with him. It's a definite possibility. But I fought this thing for all of seven days before losing my mind over him. Again. I have no impulse control when it comes to him.

"Connie, don't take this the wrong way, but you'll have to beg for my forgiveness before we even get to the sex. I just don't want to do it here." I wave a hand around the small office.

"There's a possibility you won't forgive me?" Connor assess me with those gorgeous, dark eyes.

"There's a possibility, Connor. You just have to risk it."

"It's a good thing I like risks, then."

With a kiss on my head, he tells me to wait and disappears out the door. I take my first deep breath since I saw him, and I'm assaulted by his scent. There's a mirror hanging on the wall next to me and I turn to look at my reflection. My hair is a mess, my lips are puffy and bruised, cheeks flushed, eyes wild.

"You should change your mind," I tell my reflection. "Why do you want to leave with a man who broke your heart once and can do it again?"

The door opens again before I can make up my mind either way and my sisters, Mia, and Julia enter the office.

"What is going on?" Sienna demands.

"I think I'm leaving with Connor."

"You think?" Sadie asks.

"You're here for seven days and you hook up with Connor Hayes?" Julia wonders. I'm startled for a second that she knows him before I remember that Connor used to play for the Toronto Knights. Of course, Julia knows him, she's a hockey fan.

"I'll tell you the history later," Sienna says, before turning to me. "Are you sure about this?"

"I mean, I know I want to have sex with him, but I'm not sure about anything else. Am I being crazy? You'll tell me if I was, right?"

"From the older sister POV, I saw the aftermath of him leaving you and now that I know it was him, it doesn't endear him to us," Sienna says. "But if you're sure then we're okay with it."

"I'm not ready to forgive him. I just want to have sex with him."

"He's hot, for an old guy," Mia says.

"She does have a point," Sadie agrees.

I hug my sisters and cousins. "Where are the boys?"

"They won the flirting game and proceeded to the hook up game," Julia says.

Connor is standing in the little hallway outside with my coat. He helps me put it on and buttons it up, knotting the belt.

"It's like wrapping my own present," he whispers, so only I hear him.

"Be safe," Sienna says, when I hug her. I don't think she's talking about sexual safety. I feel like I'm going off to war rather than hooking up with an ex-boyfriend. Only, Connor isn't any ex-boyfriend. He's the one I'm still in love with.

SIXTEEN
SCARLETT

The ride back to Connor's house is quiet. Snow started falling while we were in the bar, and everyone seemed to have disappeared inside. Connor keeps one of my hands in his, almost like he's afraid I'm going to jump out of the car if he lets me go.

"What if I change my mind when we get to your house?" I ask.

Connor glances at me. "Then I'll drive you right back to the Inn. Or, if you prefer, we can stay at my house and talk."

"Oh, now he wants to talk," I say.

Connor cuts me a look. "I always want to talk to you, Scarlett."

"Except when it actually matters," I retort.

He looks away, but not before I catch his flinch. I feel bad for being mean, but I have to be. I trusted him and he took advantage of that trust.

"I'm guessing you still haven't read my letter?"

"Who leaves a letter Connor? How hard was it for you to pick up a phone and call me? We were together for six months and you called and texted me more than my parents or sisters. Sometimes I worried you were love bombing me."

He looks horrified at the accusation, and it makes me laugh.

"I wasn't! I just like talking to you." *Like*, he says. "Even when you're angry at me, I just want to listen to your voice." He looks at me briefly. "*Not* in a creepy, sexualized way because of your job."

I didn't think it was creepy and sexualized, but I appreciated the clarification.

"Not that you're inclined to talk to me right now," he adds.

"Oh, so it's my fault?" I turn to him.

"No!" He squeezes my hand once and looks at me suspiciously. "This reminds of that time you picked a fight with that kid."

I gasp. "That kid was evil, Connor!"

I'm surprised he remembers. We'd been out at dinner one night and this toddler at the next table was having a tantrum and kept throwing pieces of bread at me. The parents were too busy talking and while I would never try to parent someone's child, I made an exception in that case. Only it came across as me picking a fight with a toddler.

I look at him. His face is in shadow and even though he has one hand on the steering wheel and it's snowing outside, his confidence isn't wavering. His thumb rubs circles on the back of my hand.

"I didn't think you'd remember," I say honestly.

"What do you mean?" He looks at me in question.

"I don't know why I thought you would purge all your memories of me." I shrug, looking out the window. Him leaving meant he didn't want to be with me and in my mind that meant he was going to make a concentrated effort to forget all about me, including the memories we made together.

"I will never forget you, Scarlett," he says, voice full of

conviction. "I know I haven't done a good job of proving it, but you can trust me on that. It's impossible for me to forget you when you're the reason I breathe. And I know I'm the last person you want to trust right now, but I'm going to change that as well."

"We'll see," is all I say.

"Do you always have to give me a hard time?"

"Hey, you said it yourself you're practically geriatric. I have to keep you young."

"That's why I'm dating a younger woman," he says, winking at me.

"Ugh! Gross! We're not dating." I laugh at his joke.

"We're not dating *yet*, baby girl," Connor says, turning the truck into the drive leading up to his house. House was putting it mildly. It was the kind of sprawling mansion which spoke of generational wealth. The ranch was far enough from town that he practically lived in the middle of nowhere.

"Don't you get scared living out here by yourself?" I ask, when the house appears. He's left the exterior lights on.

"I like being away from the town, and I'm not alone. Oliver lives over there." He points to a smaller structure in the distance. "It's where the ranch hands live during the summer, but it's just Oliver right now."

"And Oliver is...?"

"The ranch foreman," he explains. "He manages the day-to-day work."

"Is he cute?"

"No!"

Connor rolls the truck to a stop and puts it in park, his face set in harsh, angry lines. I giggle when he gets out and walks around the truck to open my door. Unlatching my belt, I give him my hand and Connor wraps his arm around my waist, lifting me out of the truck.

I shiver as the cold hits my exposed face and neck and Connor tucks me in against him, leading me up the steps to the porch. My heart beats wildly as I wait for him to unlock the door. I wasn't nervous in the bar, but now that we're here, I'm suddenly worried about following through. I believe Connor and I know he'll drive me back to the Inn in an instance.

We haven't had sex in a year and a half. In that time, I haven't had sex with anyone else either. I've been on a few dates but none felt like they could replace the hole in my chest left by Connor.

With the door unlocked, Connor pushes it open and steps aside, letting me enter first. I stare at the open entryway. Slowly, Connor reaches for my hand and brings it up to his mouth, kissing the back of my fingers.

"If you want to leave, or stay and talk, that's fine. I just want to be with you. I didn't bring you here for sex."

"But it'll be nice if it is sex?" I take a tentative step closer to him, tilting my head back to look into his eyes.

"Nice isn't the word I'd use to describe our sex life, but yes."

I find it so strange how he keeps referring to our relationship in the present tense. As if the last year and a half was a break and not a break-up. The way he's looking at me right now, full of desire and tenderness, I'm sure that Connor wants me back. That he'll go to any lengths to get me back and if that means spending the rest of our lives convincing me that our relationship is worth saving, then he'll do that.

I reach up onto my toes and kiss him softly.

"You'll have to beg for my forgiveness first, beg for a taste. And then I might consider letting you in."

I step into the house and Connor closes the door behind us. The sound of the door clicking shut has a finality to it.

"Do you want something to drink?" Connor asks, his voice low.

I really shouldn't drink, but I need something to calm my nerves. "I'll have whatever you're having."

I remove my coat and Connor crouches down to unzip my boots, helping me remove them one at a time. Seeing him kneeling before me sends flutters to my belly. Oh, I'm going to enjoy making him beg.

Taking my hand, he leads me into the living room where he starts a fire in the fireplace and offers me a glass of scotch. I don't drink hard liquor. I take a tentative sip and cough at the burn.

"I also have beer," Connor says.

"This is fine."

I look around the living room. There are two brown suede couches, a cream and brown Aubusson rug, and a brown leather wingback chair by the fireplace. There's a small table beside it and there's a book set upside down on it. Family photos line the mantel above the fireplace and over the piano.

"Do you play?" I ask, nodding at the piano.

Connor is watching me carefully as I examine his house.

"No, it was my mother's."

"What about your brothers? Do they play?"

He shakes his head.

Connor hasn't turned on any of the big lights. The only light in the room is from the fireplace and the floor lamps he turned on.

I take another sip of my drink and set the glass on the mantel. Outside the window, snow continues to fall. I can't see anything beyond the few feet illuminated by the house lights. It's almost like there's no one else in the world except Connor and me.

In the reflection of the window, I see him step up behind

me and brush my hair over my shoulder. Bending forward, he places a searing kiss on my neck. I tilt my head to the side to give him easier access.

"Connor," I whisper.

I turn to face him, slipping my arms around his waist. His lips meet mine in a lush, wet kiss that I feel all the way to my toes.

"I've been dying to taste you," Connor murmurs. "Five hundred and thirty-six days, baby girl. Every day has felt like a new hell."

I stare up at him. "You've counted the days we've been apart?"

Connor caresses my cheek, tucking a piece of my hair behind my ear. "Like I said, every day away from you has felt like hell. One that I brought on myself, I know. But that hasn't made it easy. The only thing which made it easy was knowing you weren't going through it with me."

What? He thinks I've been happy without him? Five hundred and thirty-six days have been easy? I want to argue, but he's kissing my neck again and I'm distracted by my need for him. I close my eyes, letting my body grow lax.

Reaching between us, Connor tugs at his shirt I'm still wearing and pulls it over my head.

"Do you want me to stop?" His eyes bounce between both of mine.

I step away from him, back towards the warmth of the fire. Slowly, I unbutton my jeans and shimmy them off with my back still to Connor, letting him see my high-cut lace thong. He makes a sound that sounds suspiciously like a whimper. Turning, I kick my jeans over to him.

I cock a hip, slowly reaching up to pull my hair up into a bun, letting Connor's heated gaze trail across my body.

"Do you want me, Connor?" I ask, my voice breathy. I'm

not putting it on like I was at the bar. This is just the Connor effect.

"More than my next breath," he says, voice roughened with desire.

"Then you'll have to get on your knees and beg for a taste."

Without a second thought, Connor drops to his knees and crawls to me. Oh, fuck. The image of him crawling towards me will be forever burned in my mind. There's something so heady about having a man get on his knees for you. It's the ultimate power trip.

"You're the most beautiful thing I've ever seen," he says, when he's kneeling in front of me.

He's looking up at me like I'm the thing he worships. Like I'll be the reason for his salvation. Bending forward, I thrust my hand into his hair, pulling his head back to give him one, hard kiss. I straighten before he can deepen the kiss and turn around.

"Can you unhook me, please?"

I'm drawing out the inevitable and the tension between us is thickening with each passing second. My pussy is throbbing with need, aching to be filled. I can't stop the sound which leaves my mouth when Connor's hands meet my heated body. They're rough and calloused as he molds them over my ass and presses a kiss against the curve of one. I shudder.

With deft fingers, he unhooks my corset, placing soft kisses along each inch of exposed skin. I let the corset fall forward and slip it off, throwing it away. I turn slowly. This time, I'm sure Connor whimpers, biting his fist. The cold air of the room causes my nipples to pebble, but the heat of the fire is nice. As is the heat in Connor's eyes.

"You're a goddess of sex and beauty sent to torture me, baby girl," he says. He's still fully dressed and I don't think he even realizes it. There could be a fire here and he wouldn't realize.

"I haven't even started with the torture yet," I tease.

Connor kisses my lower belly where my panties dip into a v. "Fucking perfect. Every single inch of you."

His hands are on my body, one gripping my waist while the other runs along my torso, and up to my breasts. Softly, he brushes the back of his fingers teasingly over my nipple. My pussy clenches in response.

Connor moves lower, tongue brushing along the edge of my panties. I use my hand in his hair as leverage to pull him back. He looks up at me in question.

"It's not going to be that easy, baby. If you want a taste, you'll have to beg."

He watches me with dark eyes. "Please."

I pout. "You can do better than that."

"Please, Scarlett. I need to taste you."

My fingers trail over his eyebrows, across his cheekbones, his straight nose, and down to his lips. I like having him at my mercy. I like the way he watches me, like I'm the only thing in the world.

"That's a good start," I whisper.

"Every day I've been away from you, it's all I thought about," Connor says. "Being able to touch you, feel you beneath me, taste you. I feel like I might die if you deny me now. Please, baby, just one taste. I've been starving for you for years, so desperate that I've half a mind to think you're not even real." He nuzzles my nipple with the tip of his nose before pulling it into the heat of his mouth and sucking gently. My hips buck forward at the sensation.

"Connor," I whimper.

"Say yes, baby girl. Jesus. Fuck. *Please,* say yes. Put us both out of our misery." His heated eyes meet mine. "I'll do anything for you. I'll spend the rest of my life kneeling before you because your body is the only thing I want to worship. Say yes."

His eyes implore me, stare straight into my soul and demand that I say yes. Not just to this moment, but to him. To every moment that comes after this. It's the first time I want to give up a fight this easily.

"Yes," I whisper.

With a groan, Connor pulls me into his lap, mouth meeting mine in a kiss. I tug at this t-shirt, our lips parting just long enough for me to pull the shirt over his head. I moan at the sensation of his bare chest against mine, the sparse hair rubbing against my nipples.

His hard length presses directly against the softest parts of me and I rock into him. Connor hisses, grabbing my hips and stilling my movements.

"You promised me a taste, baby girl," he growls.

He moves, pushing me onto my back on the rug and his hips straddled between my thighs.

"Why are you still wearing jeans?" Reaching between us, I unlatch his belt and unbutton his jeans, pushing them down. Connor kicks them off the rest of the way as he kisses my neck and down the valley between my breasts.

His fingers hook into my panties, and he removes them in one quick move, moaning at the sight of my bare pussy. Dropping to his elbows between my spread legs, he presses the flat of his tongue over my pussy, licking me all over.

"Oh, fuck," I whimper. The sight of his dark head between my legs is enough to make me come. But Connor isn't ready for that. No, he tastes me like I'm a feast, like he truly has been starving for me.

"Sweetest thing I've ever tasted, baby girl," he rasps over me. "I've been dying a slow death each day without you."

I wish he'd stop saying things like that because they mess with my head. I want to let my body take over while I keep my heart protected and he won't let me because he insists on talking about our feelings. Or his feelings, at least. I can't help but notice that he's never asked me to return them.

It's too late to think about that because Connor is feasting on me like a dying man with his last meal. He teases and sucks, his tongue swirling over my clit. I thrust a hand into his hair, holding him to me as my back arches off the floor.

"Connor," I moan. "Don't stop."

No one knows my body the way he does. He can get me to the brink of orgasm with the lightest of touches, maybe because I'm always wet and aching for him.

"I missed the sounds you make."

Slowly, he pushes two fingers inside me, and I hiss at the stretch. I haven't been with anyone since we broke up. Connor is slow and gentle, always careful as he fucks me with his fingers while his tongue plays with me.

His other hand is all over my body, feeling me, cupping my breasts, squeezing and kneading, all the while his mouth works me over.

"I'm so close," I tell him, and he laughs. The sound vibrates through my clit.

"You don't have to tell me, baby." He looks up at me from between my legs. "You think I don't remember the way this pretty little cunt tightens when you're going to come? The way you jerk your hips and grip my hair? I remember everything."

He sets his mouth back on me, sucking on my clit as he curls his fingers inside me to hit that one spot which makes me see stars. I cry out, coming in a rush, back arching off the floor as I squeeze my legs around him. Connor doesn't move. He continues to lick and suck so that one orgasm rolls into two.

I sob out his name. Connor kisses and sucks on the sensitive skin of my inner thighs and I know without looking that he's leaving marks on me.

I try to pull him up by his hair and he grabs my hand.

"Not yet, baby girl. You need to come at least one more time before you're soft enough to take me," he says.

"I hate it when you're considerate," I say, throwing an arm over my eyes.

"I'm sure the multiple orgasms are terrible," he quips, lightly biting my clit. My hips buck up towards his mouth and he laughs. It doesn't take long before I'm crying out again, coming with a ferociousness that makes me breathless.

Connor rears up to kiss me and I moan at the taste of myself on his mouth.

"See how good we taste together?" He whispers.

"I need you, Connor." I push at his boxer briefs, which he's still wearing for some reason. Reaching between us, I wrap a hand around his rigid length and oh, fuck. I forgot how big and thick he is. This is why I need to come at least three times before he can fuck me.

Connor's head drops to my shoulder and he shudders as I continue to play with him.

"You're going to make me come before I can fuck you," he says with a groan.

With a heavy, disappointed sigh, I release him. "We can't have you coming so soon. It'll be hours before you're ready to go again, at your advanced age."

Connor's head pops up and he glares at me. "That's not funny, hellion. I think you can remember being fucked to within an inch of your life and not being able to walk properly the next day."

"A year and a half ago, when you were younger," I say.

"Seems like you need to be reminded of what it was like between us," Connor says.

The head of his cock notches at my entrance and with one swift motion, he pushes in. I gasp, clinging to him, my hands splayed on his back, the full weight of his body resting on top of me. Something inside me breaks and heals at the same time.

I missed this, being connected to him this way.

Connor's eyes connect with me and I see the same emotions dancing in his eyes. The feel of him inside me is like nothing else I've ever experienced.

"Fuck, baby girl. You feel so good."

He puts an arm behind my knee, spreading me wider for him and *oh my god*, he's so deep I'm going to feel him for days.

"Fuck, how I've missed you," Connor whispers. "I've regretted every moment of the last year and a half and I'll do anything to make it better. I want to keep fucking you, just like this. Fill you up until there's no room for my cock and then lick you clean only to fill you up again. Over."

Thrust.

"And over."

Thrust.

"And over."

Thrust.

"Until I'm the only thing you remember."

The drag and push of his cock makes my eyes roll back into my head. I'm going to have a rug burn tomorrow with the force of his thrusts but I don't care. I don't care about anything other than Connor fucking me, my nails dragging down his back, marking him as mine the same way he's marking me as his.

"Yes," I hiss, when he hits a particularly good angle.

"I know you want to mark me as yours, hellion. Go ahead. Bite and scratch as much as you want."

"As if I need your permission," I snark, before biting his shoulder.

He laughs, grabbing the back of my head and holding me to him.

My hands lower, grabbing his ass and urging him to go

faster. A storm builds in the pit of my stomach and I'm going to come soon. Our sweat slicked bodies move together in the perfect rhythm as if it's been days since we last had sex and not years.

"Christ, I missed the way your eager pussy sucked me back in. Like you're empty without me."

Lowering his head, Connor kisses me, our tongues tangling as he pushes a hand between our tightly wound bodies and circles his fingers over my clit. I come with a sharpness that surprises me, my body clenching around his cock. Connor curses softly as the heat of his release fills me.

My head falls back, cushioned by Connor's hand. The sound of our hard breathing fills the room.

He pulls out of me slowly, easing his body down until his face is directly in front of my pussy. His cum drips out of me and he uses two fingers to catch it, pushing it back in.

"Oh my god!" I cover my face with my hands.

"Don't be scandalized, baby girl. Just putting it back where it belongs."

He puts his mouth back on my pussy and I yelp.

"What are you doing?" I cry out.

His grin is a wicked thing. "What I promised, Scarlett. I'm going to lick you clean before I fuck you again."

He thrusts his tongue into me, and I gasp. It's so filthy and unexpected, and it gets filthier when Connor arcs up to kiss me. I groan as he pushes our salty release into my mouth. He makes me come once again before he flips me to my stomach and pushes into me again. It's going to be a long, sore night.

SEVENTEEN
CONNOR

I'm dreaming of a warm, soft body, the wet heat of a mouth wrapped around my cock. I groan, my hips shifting and arching up to feed more of myself into Scarlett's mouth. Because who else would I be dreaming of? She loved to wake me up like this.

She swirls her wet tongue around the head of my cock and sucks on it like a lollipop. Reaching down, I settle my hand on the back of her head, urging her to go faster, and the noises she's making sound so real it takes me a moment to realize that it *is* real.

I swim up from the fog of sleep to my dark room, moonlight streaming in through the window to highlight Scarlett's lavender head sucking and licking my cock.

"Jesus Christ, baby," I say, my voice rough with sleep.

Scarlett looks up at me through her lashes as she continues to suck my cock.

"I couldn't sleep," she murmurs.

"I figured."

She's still delightfully naked as she moves up my body and kisses me. After I fucked her a second time in front of the fireplace, I made her a sandwich while she cleaned up and when she was fed, I carried her to my room and fucked her again on the bed, losing myself in the softness of her body. Scarlett has always made me feel insatiable. No matter how many times I've had her, I want more and more and more.

I grab her, urging her to straddle my hips.

"You want me to ride you the way I was planning on riding that bull?" Scarlett asks with a giggle.

"I'm the only one you ride, baby girl."

I fist my cock, guiding it to her wet heat. She's still wet from us, and I slide into her with ease. Scarlett lets out a loud moan.

"Nothing compares to the feel of your tight cunt wrapped around my cock," I tell her.

She fits me like a glove and if I could, I'd spend the rest of my life connected to her like this. Seven days ago, I never thought we'd end up here. I thought she'd never forgive me, and she still hasn't. But she's indulging in her need for me and that's a step forward.

Scarlett sits up and it forces her to take more of me. Her hair falls everywhere, and she reaches up to pull it up. The action causes her perfect tits to lift, and I arch up, taking one into my mouth, rolling my tongue over the soft flesh. The part of me which is possessive and barbaric thrills at the sight of my marks on her pale skin.

"Connor," Scarlett whimpers. "I love the way you fill me. The most delicious stretch."

I keep my hands on her waist as she starts to ride me, slowly at first, rocking back and forth, her hips undulating over me.

"I wanted you to see me up there," she says, locking eyes with me. "See the way I rode that bull. I wanted you to picture me like this, riding you in the middle of the night because I can't go another second without you inside me."

She rides me lazily, not chasing an orgasm, only a connection. When she gets a wistful look in her eyes, I fist her hair and gently pull her head back until her eyes meet mine.

"I'm yours, baby girl. However and whenever you want me. I've been yours since the moment I looked up and saw you in a crowd of thousands of people. There hasn't been anyone else since you and there won't be anyone else after you."

Gripping the back of my neck, Scarlett gives me a sloppy, sucking kiss.

"I'm still so angry," she says. "You left me without a second thought and made me feel like I didn't deserve your love. Like I didn't matter."

I know I fucked up, but it isn't until this moment that I realize the magnitude of it. I didn't just break Scarlett's heart, which is bad enough. I also made her doubt herself.

"*No*, baby." I hug her to me, foreheads resting against each other. We're having this raw conversation while she continues to shift her hips over me.

"If there's anyone unworthy in this relationship, it's me. I left to protect you because I would never have been able to give you what you deserved once I came back. I knew that my time and attention would be divided, and you deserved so much better."

"And you couldn't tell me that?" She cries out when I move and my cock hits a part that drives her wild.

"Do you know how much I love you? From the moment I saw you, I was yours. I was ready to leave my career right then and there to be with you," I tell her honestly. "The only reason I continued was because you weren't ready to have my attention on you 24/7. If you give me the chance, I'll keep you locked away, so I never have to be without you. I didn't have a choice other than to come back and I knew hearing your voice, seeing your tears would have killed me."

"You were selfish!" She bites out.

"I was," I admit. "I still am. Give me the slightest hint and you're never leaving here again."

Scarlett pushes me back and I fall onto my elbows, watching her ride me. Her face is twisted in anger, but she's too far gone in chasing her pleasure to stop now. She takes all of me with ease, her pussy clenching and releasing around me.

"I should use you," she says. "I should use you and not let you come. You don't deserve it."

"I probably don't, but you love the feel of me filling you up. It makes you feel like you're mine because you are. Look at how soft you get for me, how eager to have me fill you up and make you mine. If you weren't on birth control, you'd leave here pregnant."

Her cunt clenches around me and she exhales a breathy little moan.

Oh, fuck.

"Do you want that, baby girl?" I ask, my voice low. I suck on her pulse point, running my tongue over it and feeling her pulse throb. "Do you want me to fill you up and breed you? You'll be mine in every possible way and you'll never be able to get rid of me."

A shudder runs through her body and her movements speed up. I grab her hips, moving her up and down my shaft.

"Oh my god, Connor," she moans.

I roll my thumb over her nipple, lowering my head to take her in my mouth. Her body is so responsive, her thighs closing around me as I roll my thumb over her clit. Scarlett comes with a sweet, sharp cry of my name, her nails digging into my shoulders as she clutches me close.

Her pussy clenching around me triggers my own orgasm, my balls tightening as I hold her to me, filling her just as we both need.

I fall back on the bed, taking her with me. Our harsh

breathing fills the room. Scarlett kisses my chest, running her hands over me.

We get up long enough to clean up and when we slide into bed again, Scarlett snuggles in next to me, her head on my shoulder. I missed this more than the sex. Just holding her close, listening to the sound of her breathing. When she's with me, I experience the kind of peace I never have before.

This is what I imagine home feels like. A place I can come back to without fear and worry and will always be accepted. Perhaps that was what I felt the first moment I looked at her.

Scarlett is my home.

"I still don't forgive you, Connor," Scarlett whispers.

"I know."

But it doesn't matter anymore. I still want her forgiveness, but I know now that Scarlett still loves me. And if I have to wait the rest of my life for her to forgive me, I'll do that.

"Why don't you have any Christmas decorations up?"

"There's no one here except me," I say. "There's no one to decorate for."

Her head pops up and she rests her chin on my chest as she looks at me with narrowed eyes. "What about Jane?"

Her question surprises me. "Jane and I dated in high school, baby girl. I told you there's been no one else and I meant it."

"So it wasn't said in the heat of the moment?" A flash of vulnerability appears in her eyes.

I kiss her temple. "It was the truth. There's you or there's no one else."

She frowns, settling her head back on my chest. I'm not sure if she believes me, but it's a good thing I'm willing to convince her.

WHEN I WAKE UP AGAIN, it's to light outside. Scarlet is still asleep, her body curled against mine. The blanket is pulled all the way up over her head so only the purple of her hair is visible. Kissing the top of her head, I move, slowly shifting out of bed.

The last thing I want to do is leave her, but I should really go check up on the animals. They predicted fifty centimeters of snow last night and from what I can see out the window it's more than that.

The roads will probably not be cleared until later and I won't be able to take Scarlett back to the Inn. This wasn't my plan when I brought her back with me last night, but I'm suddenly glad she'll be stuck with me for the rest of the day.

I use the washroom in the hall, so I don't wake her and get dressed quietly.

The snow has thankfully stopped, and it takes Oliver and me roughly an hour to make sure the animals are safe and warm. When I get back to the house, Scarlett is still sound asleep. It doesn't look like she's even moved from her spot.

It's only seven in the morning and we had sex twice more last night after she woke me up the first time. She should at least be sleeping until noon.

My body is too used to waking up at the ass crack of dawn and I'm too restless to sleep. I tackle the rest of my to-do list while Scarlett sleeps.

By noon, I'm starting to get worried, so I make coffee and bring it up to her.

I find her sitting up in bed, her hair a wild mess, the blanket clutched to her bare chest. In the light of day, I can clearly see all my marks cover her body. I'm rendered stupid by how beautiful she is.

"What time is it?" She asks, voice still husky with sleep. I sit down on the bed in front of her and hand her the coffee.

"Noon."

Scarlett puckers her lips, blowing on the coffee. "I should probably call my family and let them know you haven't killed me." She takes a sip of her coffee and blinks in surprise. "You remember how I take my coffee."

"You're not a woman anyone forgets."

Gently, I push her hair behind her ear, and she hums, tilting her head into the palm of my hand.

"You're not freaking out?" I ask.

She looks up at me. "No. I know exactly what I was doing last night. Are you?"

I grin. "No, baby girl."

"You really need to stop calling me that, Connie."

I ignore that. Calling each other nicknames we pretend to hate is what we do.

"I have some bad news," I say gently.

She's immediately alert, sitting up straight. "Is it something with the wedding? I need my phone. There isn't a lot of time to fix it!"

"Calm down," I say, grabbing her arm. "The wedding is fine. It snowed a lot last night and the road isn't clear so I can't take you back to the Honeysuckle until later tonight."

Scarlett sags with relief. "That is bad news. I have to be stuck here with you the whole day. But at least the wedding is fine." She straightens again, her eyes wide. "We were supposed to go to Calgary today to meet with your florist!"

"I called her this morning and she's sent me a few options for bouquets and decorations. You can look at them afterwards."

Surprise flickers across her face. "Oh. Well, that's good. But there's still the center pieces. Sienna wanted something from Silverpine."

"I called the designer working on the lodge's redesign and

she's more than happy to supply centerpieces. She's also sent options. The lodge is also reserved for December 22nd for the rehearsal dinner. I also got your deposit back from Mel since she's no longer doing the flowers and bouquets. Your reservation at the spa has also been confirmed. Anything else?"

Scarlett pushes back her hair, looking at me through squinty eyes.

"So you just," she waves around her hand, "fucked me to within an inch of my life last night and then took care of my sister's wedding prep this morning?"

I shrug. "I didn't want you to worry." I grip her chin, tilting her head back as I lean in for a kiss.

Scarlett pulls back. "I haven't brushed yet."

"Like I give a fuck. Nothing is going to stop me from kissing you, baby girl."

I seal my mouth over hers, kissing her deeply and thoroughly, fucking my tongue into her mouth the same way I fuck her delicious cunt.

Scarlett hums with pleasure.

"You're a good kisser," she says.

"I have to be so I can keep up with you. Now, finish your coffee and I'll make you breakfast."

Her stomach grumbles on cue and she places a hand over it.

"You're not going to shower with me?" She pouts.

"If I shower with you, we're going to end up fucking."

Scarlett rolls her eyes. "Wouldn't want you to do anything you're not going to enjoy."

Tugging on her hair lightly, I nip her lip. "I don't want to hurt you, hellion. You're going to be sore enough today without me acting like a sex-starved barbarian."

She sets her coffee cup aside and stretches, letting the blanket pool in her waist. My eyes drop down to her tits, and I can't resist reaching out and brushing my knuckles over the rosy tip of one.

"But you *are* a sex-starved barbarian," she says with a satisfied smile.

I growl and throw the blanket over her head, making her laugh.

EIGHTEEN
SCARLETT

I step out of the shower and dry off, pulling on the lounge pants and t-shirt Connor left for me. Before I put on the t-shirt, I can't help staring at the marks he's left all over me. It's barbaric, but I also enjoy it because he's *my* barbarian. The same way I enjoyed him telling me that he's going to knock me up. I flush at the reminder and don my t-shirt.

Stepping out of the washroom, I pick up my phone and speak to my family, letting them know I'm alive and well, and Connor will drop me home once the roads clear. Sienna reports that Luke surprised her last night when they got back to the Inn and luckily, he managed to get in before the roads got really bad.

"So, what's this I'm hearing about you dating Connor Hayes?" Luke asks, when Sienna gives him the phone. "Do I need to fight him?"

I frown at myself in the dresser mirror. There are knick knacks scattered over the top. A half empty bottle of cologne, Connor's wallet, a couple of loonies, a five-dollar bill, his watch.

"Have you ever fought anyone, ever?" I ask.

Luke is silent for a second. "I thought I'd offer as your brother. But I can also stand back and hold your earrings while you fight him."

"Thanks, Luke. I really appreciate it," I say with a laugh.

I hang up and open one of the dresser drawers to look for socks. I find them in the third drawer and when I take a pair off the top, there's a blue box nestled amongst its brethren. My heart slams into my chest. The box is small, definitely some kind of jewelry, like earrings...or a ring.

I shouldn't check it.

I still don't know how I feel about Connor and me getting back together. But, I think I'm ready to forgive him, knowing that whatever happened, it wasn't because he wanted to leave me. It eases the burn inside my chest when I think about the last year and a half.

Because I'm apparently a masochist, I pick up the box and open it. A beautiful marquise diamond ring is tucked inside. I swallow, tempted to pull it out and try it on. I do the sensible thing and close the box, putting it back where it belongs and closing the drawer.

It's way too soon to be thinking about marriage. Last night it was children. Today it's marriage. Tomorrow I'll be deciding I want to move to Silverpine. Objectively, I can do my job from anywhere, but I can't live in Silverpine. The small town vibes are too weird for me.

I leave the room and halt in the hallway, my mouth dropping open in shock.

Connor decorated for Christmas.

Garlands hang over the banister and as I follow the stairs down, I notice there's garlands and lights around the fireplace mantel. The fake plant next to the window has been replaced with a Christmas tree which has been decorated to perfection.

The arched entry to the living room has string lights strung along it. A mistletoe hangs in the middle.

"Baby girl."

I turn to look at Connor. He's standing outside the kitchen, his hands in the pockets of his lounge pants.

"Why?"

"Because you're the only person I'd do this for. The only person I want here to celebrate the holidays with."

I don't want to cry, but I feel like I might. Tentatively, Connor walks forward, as if expecting me to lash out. He pulls me into a hug, and I wrap my arms around him, breathing in his clean scent.

I can't believe he did this for me. I can't believe he handled everything with my sister's wedding that this town messed up. But I should because this is what Connor does. He's always been good with taking care of things.

"When did you wake up?" I wonder.

"Around six."

I pull back to look at him. "Are you telling me I'm not good at sex, Connie? Because there were two people who had explosive sex all night long and only one of us needed to recover from it."

"Don't worry, baby girl. Your sex-starved barbarian is definitely going to need a day to recover."

"You say that, but if I offered sex right now, you'd take it."

Connor laughs. "I'm not dead, hellion."

He wants to marry you, my subconscious whispers at me.

Taking my hand, Connor leads me into the kitchen. He's made us breakfast for lunch; pancakes, bacon, and eggs. We sit down at the table to eat.

"Did you grow up here? In this house, I mean," I ask, looking around the kitchen.

It's modern, with cream countertops and sage green cabinet

doors. The appliances all look new, as if the place was recently renovated. The walls are painted a soft white with plenty of light coming in through the windows and backyard door.

"We used to live in town when my parents were alive," Connor says. Every time he talks about them, a sadness enters his eyes. It's been years since their death, but I imagine that's not a thing anyone gets over. I can't imagine life without my parents. "My brothers and I came to live here with my grandfather when they died."

"What was he like?" I ask.

A distant look enters Connor's eyes. "Strict. Harsh, sometimes. Difficult to deal with. Old-fashioned. He believed that a good man is one who takes care of his responsibilities without complaint. One who doesn't run away." His eyes meet mine.

"He saw my NHL career as me running away from my responsibilities, which are to this family and Cedar Creek Ranch. It's why he left me the ranch and made me the executor of my brothers trust funds. So I could never go back."

I sit back against my chair. From the way Marion and the townspeople talk about him, I thought Connor's grandfather would be some kind of saintly man. I'm sure he was a good one, but one who clearly saw the world his way and couldn't imagine anyone else's perspective being right.

"What about your brothers?"

Connor barks a harsh laugh. "I don't even know where they are. Finn is too busy partying, and Wyatt hates this family and couldn't wait to get far enough away. I'm sure Finn will come back when he gets bored and runs out of money. Should be any day now."

"WHAT ABOUT YOUR jerseys at the lodge? Hannah

suggested your grandfather hung them up," I say. Why would he hang them up if he hated Connor's career?

Connor shakes his head. "Those were gifted to him by the city council in return for some favor he did them. He had to hang them up in a prominent place."

I hate this. I hate him being trapped here with responsibilities that he didn't want. I hate that his grandfather saw his career as Connor leaving the family instead of being proud of him.

"I don't know a thing about hockey, but I am so proud of everything you accomplished, Connor," I say. "You did something you loved, and you did it well." I cover his hand with mine. "You should be proud of that, baby."

He takes my hand in his and raises it to his lips, placing a kiss on the back of it. Some darkness in his eyes disappears at my words and I realize he needs to hear them. Everyone deserves to know someone is proud of them and I don't think anyone has ever told Connor they're proud of him.

"You're taking things well," he says, as we get up to clean the plates.

"We've had sex before, Connie. Did you expect me to leave here running and screaming?"

I rinse out the plates and hand them to him to put in the dishwasher.

"Running and screaming, yes. But not because of the sex."

I shrug, crossing my arms as I lean back against the counter.

"I guess I'm just tired of fighting," I say.

"No! You, tired of fighting?" Connor looks at me with wide eyes. "I can't imagine it."

I stick my tongue out at him.

"Is that an invitation?" He asks with a smirk.

"There's the sex-starved barbarian." I look out the windows

at the snow covered Rockies. The snow is almost halfway up the house. "Are you sure they will clear the snow today?"

"Usually, they don't. But I placed a call to the council and made sure they will." Connor comes over to me, kissing the top of my head. "I know you have to get back to your family."

I close my eyes and lean into him. He thinks of everything. Including a wedding ring. My eyes pop open.

"Give me a tour of the house. I want to see where you grew up."

Taking my hand, Connor leads me out of the kitchen.

"This is the living room," he says, waving his hand around it. "And that is where you made me kneel in front of you and beg for a taste of your pussy, rewiring my brain chemistry." He points to the rug in front of the fireplace where we had sex last night.

I blush at his words. "I enjoyed that."

His heated gaze meets mine. "I did, too, baby girl."

He shows me to the den which he's using as his office, where he shows me the plans of what the lodge will look like in the next two years, he shows me the mud room, the laundry room. There's a locked door between his office and the laundry room which catches my attention.

"What's this?" I ask.

Connor looks at the door and I swear his cheeks turn a faint pink.

"It's nothing."

"Do you have a sex room in your ancestral home, Connor?"

He looks at me through narrowed eyes. "It's not a sex room." With a deep sigh, he pushes open the door and leads me inside.

Bookshelves line the walls with wide windows overlooking the front yard. There's a big, comfortable chair by the window and a couple of eclectic chairs around the room. There's another fireplace, smaller than the one that's in the living room. At first, I can't see what's in this room that will make Connor blush, but as I look around, I see it.

On one side of the room, across from the windows, is a wood structure which has a rectangular window. As I walk closer, I see that it's big enough for one person. There's a desk with a raised ledge to rest a tablet, a mike and recording equipment set up. I open the door and step inside, closing it behind me. All noise disappears. Soundproof padding covers the walls, and I guess the window is soundproof as well.

I stare at Connor through the window.

He bought me a wedding ring and he built me a recording studio in his house.

I open the door of the studio and step up, directly into his arms. Pushing up onto my toes, I grab the back of his neck and pull him down for a soul sucking kiss. He pulls me up and against him and I wrap my legs around his waist.

"This is crazy, Connor," I whisper.

"This is love, baby girl. You don't have to move here for us to be together, but on the off-chance we come back, even for a couple of weeks, I want you to be comfortable. I want you to have everything you need."

He's already decided we're going to be together. He's ready to build a life for us, whether it's here, in New York, or anywhere in the world. And I think I'm finally ready as well.

NINETEEN
SCARLETT

As Connor promised, the roads are cleared by the evening, and he takes me back to my family. Our hands are joined for the whole drive, and I get it. We spent the whole day talking and being layabouts and I don't want it to end. All the old feelings are coming back and I'm starting to realize that the Connor I loved--love--would have never left me because he didn't want me.

"Come to the ranch tomorrow morning to ride," Connor says, pressing me against his black truck in front of the Inn.

"You?" I ask, wide-eyed.

He laughs. "That's always an option, but I was talking about horses."

"Oooh, I'm sure the family will love that." I blink up at him innocently. "Do you think Oliver will be available to ride with me? I've never ridden a horse before."

I met the ranch foreman as we were leaving, and he is cute.

Connor growls, nuzzling my neck. "You'll ride with me, baby girl." He kisses me slow and deep, as if he's trying to remind me that only he kisses me like this. Like only he has the right.

"Ahem."

We pull apart to see Harvey coming down the porch steps, a shit-eating grin on her face. I smile at her, but it drops when I see Jane exiting the Honeysuckle behind her. Jane has made an enemy out of me for life for trying to destroy my sister's wedding.

"I see you two made up," Harvey says.

"I'm hard to resist," Connor replies.

"He's too pretty, so we can ignore his delusions," I say to Harvey.

"Connor, can I talk to you?" Jane asks, stepping up to us. Harvey shifts uncomfortably.

I arch up, kissing Connor's cheek. "See you later?"

"Of course. I still have to meet all my in-laws," he says, winking at me.

I laugh, walking up the steps to the Inn. When I step through the door, I feel like a different person than I was when I left it last night. I climb up the stairs two at a time and use my key to unlock the room door. It's empty, so Sadie must be in the cousins room or somewhere else. Shrugging off my jacket, I drop it on my bed and reach for my purse.

If I'm going to move forward, I need to make sure the past is in the past.

Pulling out Connor's letter, I sit down on the chair and finally open it.

Baby girl,

This isn't a letter I ever thought I would write. Once you read it, you will probably wonder why I didn't call you or see you, and the truth is, I'm too much of a coward to do either of those things. Being with you is the first time I've felt like I'm exactly where I'm meant to be. There was always this ball of anxiety in my chest that I was doing the wrong thing, chasing my dream. But that dream also brought me to you.

I'm going back to Silverpine. By the time you read this letter, I'll probably already be there. My grandfather is dying and he's requested--demanded--that I return. In a perfect world, he would understand my need for you, he would understand that I can't be happy without you. This isn't a perfect world.

I carry around too much guilt for leaving and a part of me feels like I owe my grandfather for raising three rowdy boys who just lost their parents. He's the man who taught me everything, but he's also demanding and strict, and he expects me to take over as the head of the family after he's gone. There was never another choice for me.

I want to be selfish and ask you to come with me. Don't worry, I'm not going to. I'm not going to remove you from your roots and plant you where you don't belong. I also know it's going to be a hard transition for me and I'm not going to be a good partner for you.

You'll probably hate me, and you have every right to. The choice should have been yours. But loving someone means you're willing to make good choices for them. To protect them. I hope you know that I'm protecting you, baby girl. From the town, from the bitterness of waiting for me to come back all the while knowing I can't.

I'm never going to stop loving you, Scarlett. You're not going to run into me in ten years and see me living a life without you. Without you, there is no life. I'm a creature of skin and bones, merely existing. You're the thing which gives me life.

I'm so sorry.

Always yours,

Connor

A tear splashes onto the page, and I hastily swipe at my cheek. Sadie was right. This is a love letter.

"Angel."

I blink and look up to see my family standing in the room, all wearing faces of concern.

"Hi, Daddy."

"Oh, honey, what happened?" Mom rushes forward and pulls me into a hug. "I know you shouldn't have left with him. You're so much smarter than that, Scarlett. What did Connor do?"

I hug my mother, breathing in the scent of her perfume, the same one she's worn since I was a kid. I look at the rest of my family over her shoulder.

"He bought me a ring," I find myself saying. "He keeps it in his sock drawer. He built me a recording studio in his house because even though we don't have to live here, he wants me to be comfortable when we visit. He told me I'm what gives him life."

"He broke her," Sadie says. "That's too much emotion for her to handle."

Maybe Connor did break me because I can't stop the flow of tears. I'm crying for the year and a half we missed out on. I cry for the boy who never felt his dreams were accepted.

Dad walks over and kisses the top of my head.

"She's just a little overwhelmed," Dad says.

I pull away from mom and wipe my tears, folding the letter and putting it back in my purse. I'm probably going to have to frame or put it in a plastic protector so it doesn't get damaged over the years.

AS WE DRIVE up to Cedar Creek Ranch the next morning, I realize it wasn't enough that Connor was thinking of me last night. I needed him with me, needed to feel his hands on my body.

So I'm a little eager as we get out of the car and walk towards the stable.

I see him immediately. He's got his hat on, which I left here the night before last. He's busy brushing Midnight's shiny black coat, leaning in to whisper in his ear. I admire his resilience. He never wanted to be here, but I can't deny that he's made something good of it.

"Ooh, who's that?" I turn to Mia, following her gaze to Oliver, who's working with the other horses. The ranch horseman has a forbidding, dark look about him. He's cute, but he also gives off 'don't come near me' vibes.

"Mia, he's so much older than you. He's older than *me*," I say.

She looks at me with wide brown eyes. "Connor is older than you."

"That's different. I met him when my frontal lobe had already developed. And the difference between twenty-seven and thirty-eight is a lot shorter than nineteen and whatever age Oliver is."

She twists her mouth to the side, still looking at Oliver like he's a delicious meal. Julia walks up next to her sister and while they're talking, I walk over to Connor.

"Hey, handsome," I say.

Connor turns to me, eyes sparkling with delight. "Are you talking to me or Midnight?"

"Midnight, obviously," I quip.

He growls, dipping down to kiss me.

"Are you ready to ride?"

I give him the biggest smile. "I'm always ready to ride, cowboy."

I turn as Oliver brings over the other horses and together, Oliver and Connor give everyone a lecture on what not to do while riding a horse.

We saddle up and Connor helps me swing up onto Midnight. I've never been a fan of heights and Midnight is a beast. He shifts under me, and I let out a yelp. Connor pats my thigh and Midnight's flank.

"Easy. Everything's okay."

"Who are you talking to?"

"You both."

He swings up behind me. My ass presses right against his groin.

"We're not going too far," Connor says to the group. "Follow me or Oliver and stay close."

Taking Midnight's reins, he leads us into a trot. The group follows behind us. Connor points out things as we walk, like where the staff housing is, the lodge, the property line. He tells us that once, when he was a kid, a bear casually strolled onto the property.

"Only in Canada," Sadie says. "Remember when we saw a mountain goat when we did that Banff tour?"

Sienna and I nod in remembrance.

We keep riding and I fall into the rhythm of Midnight's movements beneath me. The confident way Connor commands him. There's an icy patch and Connor tugs on the reins to stop the horse. The motion startles me and I gasp, grabbing onto his thigh.

"It's okay, baby girl. Everything's fine." Connor slips his hand through my coat and top, resting it against my stomach over the waistband of my leggings. The touch steadies me. "Just lean back into me. I won't let anything happen to you."

Behind us, I can hear everyone talking, but with Connor's hard torso behind me, his arm around me, I forget they're there.

"Connor, I keep thinking, the last-minute wedding stuff must be costing a lot of money. I know I said you have to help me, but it's going to be a while before I'm able to pay you back." I'm worried the cost is going to make my eyes bug out of my head, cartoon character style.

In response, Connor nips at my jaw, which is the only part of my upper body not covered by winter clothes. "My money is your money, baby girl. There's no one else I'd rather spend it on and if you wanted to give your sister a wedding which rivals the royals, I'd do that for you."

"I don't want your money," I argue.

"But you have it," Connor says, obstinately.

He was paid millions in the NHL and there's generational wealth involved here. We had this same argument when he bought me a Cartier watch for my birthday, three months into our relationship. The watch is delicate, the face and band inlaid with small diamonds, not the kind of thing I can wear every day.

"Connor--"

My words are cut off when he slips a hand into my leggings and panties.

"You'll let me take care of you," Connor says against my ear, his fingers teasing me. "You won't complain when I spend money on you, on things which make you happy, on things I know you want but will never ask for."

As he talks, he lowers his fingers and gently pushes them inside me.

"I know you like that, baby girl. Your pussy is dripping wet."

I bite my lip. It's less the idea of him taking care of me financially and more just him taking care of me. Something about him thinking about me all the time makes me really hot.

One of my sisters or cousins asks him a question, which he answers without a change in his voice. Like this isn't affecting him at all, when I have the evidence pressed against my ass. For the rest of the ride, Connor keeps fucking me with his fingers but just enough to drive me crazy and not come. He keeps me on the edge and each time his thumb accidentally brushes my clit, I have to bite my lip to keep from making a noise.

Once we're back in the stables, Connor invites everyone to come to the lodge for lunch, which we accept. I stay behind to help Connor with the horses while Oliver takes everyone else to the lodge. As soon as they are out of sight, I jump him.

"You can't just tease me and then head off to lunch," I say, before kissing him.

Connor groans, gripping the back of my head and tilting it to give him better access to my mouth. My hands are on his body, unbuckling his belt and unhooking his jeans.

"Someone can come back," he says.

"I don't care." I'm dying for him; I have been since last night. I pull away from him. "I read your letter."

Connor freezes, eyes bouncing between mine. "Oh?"

I lick his bottom lip. "I still think you should have called me, but I understand why you did what you did. I *don't* support it. Don't mistake my understanding for support. I would appreciate it if you can just talk to me in the future and if you do something like this again, we're done."

The biggest grin spreads across his lips, his eyes like sparkling gemstones.

"I'm never letting you go, baby girl," he promises.

He presses me against the wall of a stall, lifting me to wrap my legs around his waist.

"Too many clothes," I complain.

"We should go back to the house."

"Too far."

I quickly remove my upper layer of clothes. Connor turns me, pressing my front to the wall and then I feel him. The head of his cock notching at my entrance and he comes inside in a forceful thrust, stretching me with his thick cock. I let my head fall forward to rest on the wall as Connor rests his head on my shoulder.

He doesn't move and I don't urge him to. We stay like that, reveling in our connection.

"I need you more than my next breath," he says.

"You have me," I whisper.

He grasps my wrists with both hands, holding them above my head and he grips my hip with his other hand as he pulls out and thrusts deep. I gasp, body jerking forward with his movements, but he's got me trussed up against him.

"You don't understand how desperate I am, Scarlett. I'm a starving man without you."

My throat tightens. "Connor."

His name is a whisper lost in the wind.

His cock plunges into me again and again, our sounds filling the stable. The only sounds I hear are his words of lust in my ear, his groans, and pleasure. My clit throbs with the need to come, but I don't touch myself. I want to elongate this moment as much as possible.

Connor doesn't feel the same way because he reaches around, rolling his thumb over my clit. My body spasms, core clenching around him as I come with a loud cry of his name. Connor follows, spilling into me with powerful bursts, his groan filling my ears.

He removes his t-shirt, uses it to clean me up as best he can as I blush furiously.

Once our clothes are back in the right place, he cups my face, tilting my head back to look at him.

"I love you, Scarlett."

"Is the ring for me?" I ask, suddenly getting this niggling worry in the back of my mind that it's for someone else.

Connor blinks in surprise. "You saw it?"

"When I was looking for socks," I say with a nod.

Sighing, he kisses my temple, pulling me against him. "I bought it a month before I left."

"You were going to propose when we hadn't been dating for six months?" I ask, incredulous.

"When you know, you know, Scarlett." He looks down at me. "And I knew from the first moment I met you."

When he says things like that, it's hard not to tell him I love him, so I do just that.

"I love you, too."

TWENTY
SCARLETT

After months of waiting, the day has finally arrived. I watch my sister in the mirror as the make-up artist does her make-up, the photographer buzzing about the room. Sadie and I are sitting in chairs by the windows in our silk robes, sipping champagne.

"Just think, Scarlett can be the next one getting married here," Sienna says. "We can make it a family tradition."

"I'm not getting married in Silverpine," I say.

Most of these people might be nice, but I can't imagine living here permanently. That hasn't changed over the last few days I've spent with Connor. Being blissfully in love doesn't mean I'm ready to uproot my life for Connor.

"But you are getting married," Mom asks. She's standing behind Sienna, supervising the make-up artist.

I raise my left hand. "I don't see a ring on this finger."

"That's because it's still in Connor's sock drawer," Sadie counters. "He's probably waiting for Sienna's wedding to be over before he proposes."

I'm sure he is. Sienna has invited him, Harvey, and Marion to the wedding because we have a giant ballroom and fifty guests' total. They're mostly family and friends of Luke and Sienna's who were able to fly out.

We finish getting ready and get our pictures taken. Sienna chose black dresses for Sadie and me, as bridesmaid and maid of honor. The color is simple and classy. While Sienna finishes getting ready, Sadie and I head to the lodge, taking Sienna's dress with us. We decided it would be better if Sienna had her hair and make-up done at the Inn, which we can always touch up later. But if the dress gets dirty? There's no fixing it.

"I don't think Silverpine is so bad," Sadie says, looking out the window. "Are you and Connor going to move back to New York?"

"I don't know, Sadie. We got back together a few days ago. We haven't talked about it, yet."

Connor did build a recording studio in his house for me, but he also said we're not obligated to live here permanently. I have dual citizenship, so I'm not worried about going back and forth.

"He'll probably live anywhere you ask him."

I don't doubt it.

We get to the lodge and hang Sienna's dress in the room Harvey has dedicated for us.

"Do you want to see the ballroom?" Harvey asks, smiling at me.

"Yeah, let's go."

When she leads us into the room, my jaw drops. Flowers and string lights wrap around the wooden pillars and archways, drop lights strategically hanging from the ceiling. The aisle has waist length columns along it, also wrapped in flowers, with three candles resting on each platform. An arch of flowers and lights is set up at the end of the aisle, in front of the windows looking at the Rockies.

The ballroom is going to be used for the wedding and

reception. Harvey confirms that the staff has been instructed on that.

"It's like something out of a fairytale," Sadie says, looking around wide-eyed.

"Sienna is going to love this," I say.

"Connor had a fun time with the wedding bible," Harvey says with a laugh.

My gaze snaps to hers. "He has the book?!"

Harvey smiles softly, squeezing my hand. "He wants to do things right, and you should let him."

I'm more than willing to make Connor work for it. I just can't picture myself in a white dress, walking down an aisle, not even to him.

MARRIAGE LOOKS good on my sister. She hasn't stopped grinning since she and Luke said I do. They're swaying softly to the music that's clearly meant for dancing, which the rest of our families are doing.

I'm leaning against a pillar, watching my sister and new brother-in-law enjoy the first few moments of their married life.

"They look good together."

I turn around to see Marion behind me.

"They do," I agree.

"Maybe one day it will be you and Connor up there," she says.

I give her a strained smile, the same one I've been giving everyone who's said the same thing to me the whole day. Somehow, being in love automatically means we're getting married. Which I'm not opposed to. Hell no, I want that ring on my finger and more importantly, I want a ring on Connor's finger.

I just don't want this. I don't want fifty people watching me marry Connor. If Connor invites any of his old teammates, it's going to be more than fifty people. It's my worst nightmare.

"I'm happy you forgave him," Marion continues. "I know that wasn't easy for you."

I look at Connor across the room, talking to Logan, my cousin. Connor in a suit is sexy as fuck. He's trimmed his beard, his hair has been pushed back, he looks delicious. His eyes meet mine and he winks at me.

"It wasn't easy, no," I admit. "But I'm trying to be more understanding."

"He's exactly the same as Fred raised him," Marion says, referring to her husband. "But sometimes I wish he was a little easier on the boys. Maybe they would have been happier." She sighs, patting my arm. "I don't want to bring down the mood. I'm going to run across the hall to the Christmas party."

I smile at her even as I inwardly roll my eyes. Jane is hosting a Christmas party in the smaller ballroom. Apparently, that day she asked to speak to Connor, she was inviting him to the party, and he denied. Even though we hadn't invited him to the wedding at that point, either.

Connor walks across the room, swooping down to place a kiss on my cheek.

"You look happy," he says.

"I am," I agree. "Sienna looks beautiful and happy. The wedding went off without a hitch. The place looks gorgeous. Thank you for that, by the way."

"You don't have to thank me, baby girl," he says, kissing me softly. "But if you insist, you can do it tonight when we're alone."

"The office is closer," I say.

He laughs. "And you call me a sex-starved barbarian."

"Well, I am leaving in a few days, so..." I shrug.

Connor's smile drops. "Right."

"I can extend my trip until the new year, but I do have to go back eventually."

"That should give me enough time," he says.

"To do what?"

"Talk to Oliver about managing things here while I'm with you. There's no way I'm letting you go now."

I remember his letter and the guilt he always felt leaving his responsibilities. I don't want him to feel guilty because of me.

"What about your brothers and Marion? You have to take care of them," I say.

Eyes softening, he takes my hand and leads us onto the dance floor. "We'll figure it out. And we don't have to do it all tonight."

I put the worries out of my mind for tonight. I know tomorrow morning; I'll go back to worrying about where we're going to live and how often we will have to travel back and forth. I haven't met his brothers, and they can hate me, like half this town. I wouldn't be able to ignore them like I can this town.

But I don't worry about all that. I let Connor's arms surround me and feel his heart beating against mine. I lose myself in the feel of his lips pressing against mine, our laughter as he dips me. I lose myself in my family's happiness around me because in the end, that's all that matters.

I WAKE up on Christmas morning with my limbs wrapped around Connor. I go on a run with Connor following me in his truck and I'm struck with a reminder of telling dad that he'll be the one keeping me safe forever.

As I run, I think about waking up here every morning and going for a run. Of days spent with Connor, Harvey, and

Marion. Looking up at the Rockies every day and realizing how insignificant we are in nature.

"What are you thinking?" Connor asks, after we come back home, and I've showered and changed. Home. This place can be my home.

"I'm thinking about what it will be like to live here," I say honestly.

His eyebrows shoot up. "You don't have to move here, Scarlett."

Taking a sip of my coffee, I let my eyes drift to the view out of the windows.

"But this is your home, just like New York is mine. You have responsibilities here and I don't want you to feel guilty for leaving someone else to take care of them."

Connor sets his cup down and turns me to face him, his eyebrows dipping down in a frown. "Don't ask me to let you go. I'll live through a thousand hells before I let you go again."

"Connor, please tell me I'm not going to come home one day to you covering the walls with my photos," I say.

"It's a possibility," he says.

Shaking my head, I arch up onto my tiptoes to kiss him. He's so much taller, I have to go all the way onto my tippy toes.

"I love you, Connor. I'm not asking you to let me go," I say. "I'm suggesting we can split our time between New York and here, or Toronto, if you think that's easier. I'm a city girl, I can't live here permanently but I can't deny that Silverpine doesn't have a certain charm."

"New York is fine," he says gruffly. "I want you to be with your family."

I hug him, settling my head on his chest while Connor rests his head on top of mine.

"Connor, what's in your pocket?"

"It's nothing."

I pull away to look at him, raising an eyebrow. Sighing, he pulls out the ring box.

"Were you going to propose at breakfast with my family?" I ask.

"No!" He looks at me wide-eyed. "I know you, baby girl. I wouldn't make a spectacle out of the proposal. You don't even have to tell anyone or wear the ring." The tops of his cheeks turn red and feel a surge of love for him.

"I don't have anything to tell anyone," I say, shrugging.

"Baby girl, if you want to give people something to talk about, you only have to ask."

"I believe you have to do the asking."

Without a word, Connor drops down to one knee.

"You don't have to do that," I say.

He grins up at me lasciviously. "I like being on my knees for you. I know I fucked up our relationship, baby girl. I don't take this second chance lightly and I don't want to fuck this up. It doesn't matter if you say yes, no, or not now. It doesn't matter if we never get married. I'm going to love you with every part of my being every single day. I'm going to wake up the happiest and most grateful man alive because you love me back. Will you promise to be mine forever, Scarlett Monroe?"

A tear trickles down my cheek, and I wipe it away, nodding hastily.

"I promise to be yours, Connor Hayes."

With the biggest grin on his face, he slides the ring onto my finger. It's a perfect fit and the diamond sparkles when it catches the light. Standing up, he gives me a bone-melting kiss.

When we get to the Inn to have breakfast with my family and Marion, my mother's and sisters' eyes land on the ring immediately and they utter the loudest, most embarrassing squeal.

"Keep that up and only dad and Luke will be invited to the wedding. We only need two witnesses, anyway," I say.

"Don't worry, I'll make sure you have the most understated wedding of the century," Sienna says, clapping her hands in excitement. Luke grins, kissing her temple.

"I know you're excited, babe, but remember this is Scarlett's wedding," he says.

"I'm so happy for you both," Marion says.

As the rest of them start making wedding plans already, I turn to dad, who hasn't said anything. "Are you happy, daddy?"

"I should be asking you that," he says, clearing his throat.

Under the table, Connor squeezes my hand. "I'm happy."

"I don't know what I'm going to do without you, Angel."

"You're not getting rid of me that easily. I'm engaged, I'm not moving."

I rest my head on his shoulder, and he kisses the top of it. I thumb my ring, glancing down at it. It feels unreal. In two weeks, I went from hating men because of Connor to being engaged to him. I watch him laugh at something mom says, and I can't stop smiling as he absentmindedly lifts my hand to kiss the back of it.

I'm not a person who believes in miracles. But I can safely say the greatest miracle and gift of the season has been us finding our way back to each other.

EPILOGUE
CONNOR

Six months later

I'm fixing a fence on the north side of the property when my wife finds me. I'm shirtless, the June sun beating down on my back. Scarlett comes up behind me, wrapping her arms around my torso.

"I've been looking everywhere for you," she says.

I drop the hammer, turning to face her. She's wearing shorts, a tank top, and my hat. She was wearing something similar last night when I peeled the clothes off and fucked her in her studio.

"You were recording, and I didn't want to disturb you," I say.

"Especially since you did a bang up job of disturbing me last night."

I grin. "Did you catch up?"

Her eyes sparkle up at me. "I did. Although your brother came in looking for the lodge plans."

I sigh, rolling my eyes at the mention of my brother.

Scarlett and I got married two months ago in New York. The wedding was exactly as Scarlett wanted, with just our families. The only people not related to us were Harvey, Roman, and Lavinia. The most unexpected guest was my brother Wyatt. I'd spoken to Finn about the wedding as well, but he hadn't seemed enthused.

There wasn't any fuss or planning involved with our wedding. We got married in city hall and Scarlett didn't have to walk down an aisle. She didn't even have to wear white. Instead, she wore a pale blue backless dress, and she was the most beautiful bride, and I was the luckiest man alive.

"He'll leave once he gets bored," I tell Scarlett.

Wyatt is currently interested in the renovations for the lodge and came back with us. "At least he's not living here," I add.

"It would be pretty awkward coming home to your brother and sister-in-law having sex in the living room."

I laugh, wrapping an arm around her shoulder as I lead us back to our house. Scarlett wraps her arm around my middle, squeezing my side.

"Are you all packed?" I ask.

We're leaving for our honeymoon in two days. With the renovations on the lodge starting, we couldn't take a honeymoon earlier, but I'm determined to give us one. Just Scarlett and me, the endless ocean of the Cote d'Azur and endless hours of making love to my wife.

"I still don't understand why we need clothes on a honeymoon, but yes, I packed."

We enter the house, and I press her against the closed door, sealing my mouth over hers. Waking up to her everyday still feels like a dream. This is the life I wanted for me, which was any life with her. It doesn't fit into the life my grandfather expected, but I feel no guilt over that anymore.

"I love you, baby girl," I whisper the words against her mouth, making her breathe them in.

Scarlett grins, lighting up my whole world. "I love you, too, Connie."

ABOUT THE AUTHOR

Ava Hill has been a romance addict since high school when she discovered her first book boyfriend and found they make better soulmates.

Now, instead of reading about fictional men, she has turned to writing her very own swoon worthy book boyfriends.

Other than dreaming of fictional men, she can be found day dreaming about travelling to gorgeous locations.

Join her newsletter to be the first to know all the exciting information about upcoming projects, bonus scenes and more!

Let's be friends!

Printed in Dunstable, United Kingdom

75036264R00102